Praise for
The Man Who Built the Cross
· · · · · ·

"I really enjoyed this book! It was very inspiring. I never thought about the fact that the cross had to be made by someone, and this story had ideas I never would had considered in a million years. I loved how Josiah watched stories directly from the Bible actually happening. I would definitely recommend this book to anyone interested in a good book."

—Alli Weber, age 14
Duluth, Minnesota

"Everyone wishes they could go back in time and change something they wish they hadn't done. *The Man Who Built the Cross* brings us into the world of the Bible and the life of Josiah. You will experience the guilt and anguish Josiah felt since one of his crosses was procured to kill the Christ! You may envision the flashbacks he experiences as he tries to make sense of his life. This amazing book will draw your attention clear to the unexpected finale."

—Lorraine Simpson, licensed educator (retired)

THE MAN WHO BUILT THE CROSS

THE MAN WHO BUILT THE CROSS

MICHAEL D. GOLDSMITH

Published in the United States of America

ISBN: 978-1-7903-9199-8
Fiction / Christian / General
16.09.23

Dedicated to the Lord Jesus Christ

On May 25, 1974, Jesus the Christ started a
work in me that goes on to this day. I credit the
change he made in my life on that day, when I
was nineteen years old. Everything that has
happened wonderfully in my life to this point.

Contents

• • • • • •

1
. . . . . .
The Walls Come Crashing Down

Josiah was sleeping soundly. Suddenly the pounding on his door would start. The Roman soldiers stormed into his house shouting for him to get up.

The officer screamed, "Do you have a cross ready? We have orders to prepare an extra crucifixiontonight forthemorning."

Josiah, still in a fog from being in a deep sleep, stumbled through the house to deal with the unruly soldiers. "Who is the criminal tonight?" he asked.

The centurion looked at him and said, "Jesus ofNazareth."

Josiah's head snapped around involuntarily. "Who?"

"Jesus of Nazareth," the officer answered in an off handed manner. Then another gruff command came his way. "Are you going to get us that cross, or are we going to nail you to one?"

Josiah's mind was racing. He had been one of the people who had listened to some of Jesus' teaching and just thought to himself. *This teaching is so new. Love your neighbor as yourself? Give and it shall be given to you? The only thing I have ever done is taken. I have made a lot of money building those death trees, I haven't wanted to see someone die on one these, but for whatever reason I have to see this.*

He took the men out to the back barn where he built death trees. They found one of dogwood, strong and straight and would not fold under the weight of a man struggling for life. They paid him thirty pieces of silver for the death tree.

The officer looked at Josiah and said, "Sleep well." Then they all left.

Josiah looked around; all was quiet. He felt a dreading in his soul. *What have I done? I have just provided the death tree that is going to kill an innocent man. What have I done?* He walked around his house, back and forth, upstairs and down. He washed his hands, but they did not feel like they would ever come clean. Josiah tried to sleep, but sleep would not come. He knew what he had to do. He understood that he had to go to the hill, stand under the cross, and ask this man to forgive him. With that he went to his closet, put on a clean robe, and headed for the hill. He had no idea what he should expect; he just had to go to the hill.

Josiah wandered out into the dark. It was the middle of the night. The streets were a mass of people. He did not want to go and see that which he made destroy an innocent life, yet he was drawn with such power he had to go. He looked up to heaven, and screamed. "God! Why me? Why did I create such a hateful thing just to make money? Why?" He dropped to his knees and cried.

With his arms crossed and eyes buried in his hands, sobbing uncontrollably, the thought kept going through his mind. *God, if you're there, why did you allow me to build such a cruel tool of destruction?* He stood, looked at his hands, and started to walk toward Golgotha. The crowds were like nothing he had ever seen before. They were angry and vulgar. He had seen many of them when the Christ made his entry just a few days prior. "Hosanna!," they cried. As he came into town they cried in desperation, "Hosanna to the son of David!" Their desperate cries for salvation rang out. But now they wanted him dead. Josiah just did not understand how they could be so cruel. He pushed his way through the crowd as he kept walking up the hill to where they were going to drive nails fastening the Christ to the cross that would ultimately kill him. He was in a state of panic. Going through his mind were ideas how to get him off the cross. He knew they would not work, but his mind was racing out of control. As the night turned into day he was about to see how quickly people could change.

Then he heard that scream he had heard so many times before. He knew they had just driven the first nail. He did not know who they were driving it into, but he knew they were driving nails. He felt a sickness in his stomach. He knew what had just happened. He knew the death tree that he had built was being used to destroy the man who had brought nothing but hope to so many people.

* * *

His mind went back to the sweet smile of Anna as she talked of the Christ. His mind went back to the reaction she had when she saw the crosses he had built. He began to weep so hard his whole body shook with an emotional pain that could not be comforted.

He had heard him teach, he had seen him bring people back from the brink. He had seen him protect a woman caught in her sin without even protecting her. All he said was, "Let him who is without sin cast the first stone." Now he stood beneath the cross. He saw the blood running from his hands, his feet, and his brow where they had crowned him with thorns. Then his thoughts returned to his own actions. I did this; I built this hateful cross that they nailed him to. They paid me my thirty pieces of silver for another cross. When I built it I thought it was just another cross, but it was *thee* cross that would kill a man who just loved people. His only crime was he wanted peo-ple to understand what God's love was really like. He just wanted them to understand who his Father really is.

* * *

It was twelve noon. Jesus had already been on the cross for three hours. The sun should be beating down, but the sun had disappeared. Thick clouds had enveloped the whole area. He had never seen such darkness. Josiah thought of the souls of men who could do such terrible things. The darkness was as if he was looking into their dark souls, and his own as well. He thought more of his own soul and the darkness that must be in his soul to build such a terrible tool. He felt the earth shaking under his feet. He saw the earth split. Then Josiah heard the words.

"Father, forgive them, for they know not what they do."

Josiah's mind was spinning. He was panicked. He did not know how to get the Christ off the tree that he had built. Then he heard the words, "It is finished." He looked up and the Christ was dead, his head hanging. Josiah then saw something that turned his stomach even more. A soldier walked up to the body hanging on the cross and ran a spear into his side. Not a sound, as blood and water rushed out. Then they put ladders up against the cross and released the dead Christ from the cross. They lowered the body to the ground. They wrapped the body and headed for the tomb of a man named Joseph.

Josiah followed at a distance. His head ached; he had a pit in his stomach. Something totally inhuman had just happened to the one man who seemed to have nothing but good in him. He followed them to the tomb. Soon in the west the sun was setting and darkness was about to set in. Josiah kept saying to himself, "Why God? Why would you let me make such a cruel, hated, inhuman way of killing people?" As the darkness started to envelope him he could not go home to his dwelling place, instead he followed them to the tomb and set himself next to a rock to sleep on the ground. He did not understand why. The Christ was dead. He had no reason to be there except to listen to the sound of death. The absolute silence of death was all that could be heard. Not a cricket. Not a breeze as the night was still. Death was in the air. Sleep overtook him. Josiah fell into a deep, sound sleep.

*   *   *

Saturday morning, he woke to the same silence he had fallen asleep to. He looked at the cold stone that had been rolled in front of the opening of the grave. He wept. He looked to heaven and screamed!, "God, if this was your son, why did you let him get killed this way? Why did you not stop it?" As he shook his head he walked away. Josiah vowed, "I will stay here at the grave one more night."

Josiah walked the streets aimlessly the whole day . He could not seem to shake the funk that he was in. His insides ached from the grief that he felt. Thirty pieces of silver was what the Romans paid him for the cross. He watched the Christ bleed and die for thirty pieces of silver. He walked for hours just trying to make some sence of what happened. He passed the castle David lived in. He walked past the temple. He looked inside the Temple at the Holy of Holies. The curtain was torn in two. It had been torn the second the Christ died. "But why?" Josiah asked himself.

He stood there gazing into the Holy of Holies. The veil was torn. He could see the altar, the Ark of the Covenant, and wondered, "Why did this happen? The only ones who are supposed to see into there are the high priests." He then realized that God himself had this place built to be a dwelling place for his Holy Spirit. Josiah walked outside into the hot afternoon air of Jerusalem. He sat on a rock and looked out over the city. He could smell the fragrances, he could hear the sound of commerce in the city, and he wondered why this all happened.

"Why had they killed this good man? And why had I made the hundreds and hundreds of crosses that killed so many other men?"

He walked out of the temple. His mind was not able to comprehend what had really happened. Yet he knew the power that had been demonstrated at the death of the Christ was a power like no mere man could wield. He walked and found a huge rock just outside the temple where he would sit for hours trying to figure out what he had done.

Josiah got up from the rock that he sat on and started to walk back toward the tomb where they had buried the body of the man called the Christ. The walk to the tomb took about twenty minutes. As he arrived at the tomb, he noticed the soldiers standing guard. He sat on a log and his mind started to go back in time to before he built the crosses. To a time when he was trying to figure out what he was going to do with his life. This was a time when life was exciting. He had no trade to speak of, yet he was able to find work in many places. Day work mostly, yet an honest living. He was not getting rich, but was earning an honest living and he could take some pride in helping the rich land owners with their crops. It was hard, back breaking work, but he enjoyed the joking and fun he was able to have with the other workers while they accomplished their assigned tasks. Then he remembered an event when he worked in those fields before Christ death.

He was working with his friends in a land owner's field. Some Roman soldiers walked up. They asked if any of them would like to make some real money. All the workers were willing to listen. Then they found out it was to make killing trees. No one was willing to do it except Josiah, when he found out he would be paid thirty pieces of silver for each cross he built. He walked out of the field and bought an axe. He cut down his first cedar tree, laid it out, debarked it, and cut it square on both the long and short parts. He put it together and waited for the Romans to show up and take a look.

The chief centurion looked at the death tree and smiled.

"This is great work," he said. "Built very sturdily, they won't be able to squirm their way off of this. It will kill criminals quite nicely."

Josiah thought to himself, with a sense of self-justification way, *I am having a role in ridding the land of bad guys and will make more money building one cross than I would work in a field for a year.* Little did he know the only ones who would be put to death on his crosses were Jews, his own people. That night he went to bed thinking of all the things he could do with the money he would make building the death trees.

2

From Rags to Riches,
But at What Cost?

· · · · · ·

The next morning he woke and looked over at his money pouch. Usually there would be a few denari in it. Today there would be 30 pieces of silver, he thought to himself. He thought to himself, *"Josiah you are a man of fortune, you are helping put the dregs of the earth to death, and getting paid a small fortune to do it. Life does not get any better than this."* As he started to walk out, the Roman governor's assistant came to Josiah's door. "We need one tomorrow; can you have the tree ready?" he asked.

Josiah responded quickly. "Absolutely, it will be ready by sun up."

Instead of heading to celebrate the first killing tree he started to build his second. Josiah followed the same procedure. Cut down a cedar tree, scraped off all of the bark.

When the Romans had returned the next morning, it was ready. Once again he received thirty pieces of silver and they had their killing tree. Josiah thought he was going to be very happy. He had justified to himself what he was doing, or so he thought.

One day as he walked out of his house he heard a blood-curdling scream. He wondered what it could be. He asked a friend walking down the street if he had heard the scream. The reply stopped Josiah cold in his tracks.

"Yes, I did. You have to know, it's a crucifixion, and it's when they drive the first nail into a guy's hand. The pain about kills the guy being nailed to the death tree. It's not really a pretty sight."

Josiah nodded to his friend and turned and walked toward the closest inn. He needed something to calm his nerves. He knew he built the death tree that person was being nailed to. He had to find a way of escape from the horror that he had helped to create, but how? He walked into the inn. Josiah ordered a meal and a glass of wine. As the drink started to have its effects, he felt the pain subside. He drank and drank until he could no longer feel the pain. Dragging himself out, he stumbled back to his humble abode. He looked at the floor, laid on his mat, and went to sleep.

* * *

The next day being the Sabbath, there would be no one put to death. Josiah walked out and headed for the temple. This day there would be a man teaching there named Jesus. He would read from Isaiah. He would claim that prophecy was fulfilled in him. Josiah saw the terrible anger in the eyes of the Pharisees and Sadducees and he thought to himself as he walked away shook his head, *This will not end well for him.* He looked back. The man called Christ looked at him, and their eyes met. The intensity and power in his gaze acted like a magnet drawing Josiah back to himself. Josiah could not understand what was with this man. *How and why did he have such power?* Stroking his beard in wonderment, he forced himself to turn and walk away.

Arriving at his home, he saw a letter nailed to his door. They needed another cross. He smiled as he thought, *Another thirty pieces of silver.* He went to work cutting the cedar then removing the bark from the tree so it would be ready to be turned into the instrument it was intended for. Then he had to trim the trunk so it was a perfect square so as to stand and support the man who would be nailed to it.

For a short term he was able to put the thought of what he was doing out of his mind. The next morning he had ninety pieces of silver. He was heading to the banker to put his money in the bank. He heard it again. A bloodcurdling scream as he walked out of his home. He knew what it was. He tried to cover his ears but it was too late. He turned and looked straight into the eyes of the man named Jesus, the one they called the Christ. Jesus's kindness shone through the deepness of his brown eyes as he looked at Josiah, causing him to look away from Christ's gaze. It seemed to Josiah that Jesus was looking into his very soul and seeing the darkness within. Josiah asked himself, "*Who is the man who can see into a person's* soul? When I look into his eyes, it's as if I am looking into the eyes of God himself. But he is a mere man, and being a mere man he cannot be God."

Josiah walked over to the bank, deposited his money, and kept some for starting to live the high life.

"Wine, women, and fun are what my life will look like," Josiah said with a tone of selfishness in his voice.

As he walked down the street he saw average people milling around. People who worked day in and day out to make enough money to buy bread for their families. He thought to himself, *All I have to do is make crosses. Sure, people are going to die on the crosses I make. But I do know they deserve it. Society is better off without the dregs of the earth. Society rids itself of its garbage and I get rich doing it. It's all good.*

* * *

The following day things were calm, or so Josiah thought. He heard a huge commotion. He looked to his right and saw a crowd of angry men and one young lady. Josiah did a double take and saw she was naked. The men were cursing at her, yelling at others to stone her.

Just then the Pharisee yelled, "There is Jesus, let's ask him if we should stone her? After all, that's what the Law of Moses said to do."

Josiah followed far enough behind not to be noticed. They threw the young lady down at his feet; as they did they threw dirt in her face. She was crying in fear and in pain.

Jesus was standing there with the woman at his feet. The anger in the crowd was at a level that was really frightening. Josiah could hear the gentleness in his voice. That gentleness changed to one of a question as well as a demonstration of power with the same words.

The religious leaders had accused her of adultery. They demanded that he answer them as they said, "You know what the law says. A woman caught in adultery is to be stoned. What do you say?"

Josiah sat there astounded as he saw the Christ look at the young lady. Then he heard the Christ say, "Let him who is without sin cast the first stone."

Then as he saw the Christ kneel and write in the dirt, he really could hardly believe what he saw. The crowd was leaving. Then again he heard more words from the man they called the Christ, say to the woman, "Go your way and sin no more."

Josiah listened to Christ. The comfort yet authority in his voice had him shaking his head. *Where does this man get such power?* he thought to himself.

He turned to walk away from the scene that was before him. He just about walked into a Roman soldier.

"We have been looking for you all over Jerusalem," the soldier said gruffly. "We need a cross by tomorrow morning."

Josiah looked over to the Christ. His eyes connected with the eyes of Jesus, and once again he felt as if this man called the Christ was looking into his heart. He knew the man who had just saved a woman caught in adultery knew exactly who Josiah was and what his deepest thoughts were. Josiah was in such a hurry to get away from the penetrating eyes of the Christ that almost fell over the soldier telling him again to have the cross ready by dawn tomorrow.

Josiah looked at where the sun was in the sky. He realized he had only a couple of hours to get work done before he would have to stop for the night. Under Jewish law all work had to stop at sundown. He worked feverishly to get the tree stripped so in the morning he would square it up and get it ready for its gruesome task. Josiah had worked over and over to put out of his mind that the pain and suffering he was helping to inflict was for his own people. He also understood that most of the people who were put to death deserved it. But he also knew the Romans could put just about anyone on these crosses that they wanted to. As he worked on the death tree, the thoughts kept going through his mind that merely speaking against Caesar was enough to get a person nailed to one of those trees. He shook his head and kept working.

The next morning, the Romans came for their cross. He handed it over to them and received his thirty pieces of silver. He looked into the bag, pulled out a piece, and dropped it. He shook his head. It looked blood red to him. He asked himself, *Is God trying to show me something here?* The answer was obvious to him. The answer became clear. The problem was he was not sure how to remove himself from the highly profitable death trees that he had become extremely proficient in creating. He started pacing around his house. He raised his head toward heaven. He screamed, "God, why me? Why did I allow myself to be drawn into building these terrible death trees?"

He walked over and looked again at his money bag. The coins were silver, not red. He reached inside and pulled one out, it was red. He became sick to his stomach. He almost threw up. Josiah walked down the street to the inn, went inside, and started to drink. As he drank he could hear the agonizing scream of the man from a few days ago. And then his thoughts went to the Christ. Those eyes, they seemed to look right through him and into his soul. Who was that man? He seemed so gentle. Yet the leaders of the Jews hated him. Yet, he really seemed to be drawn to this man called the Christ. He knew he had to talk to him, to really understand who he was and what he was about. His mind went to the eyes of the man they called the Christ that would look into the deepest part of his heart. Just then he felt a hand upon his shoulder. It was a Roman soldier. He wanted another cross. Josiah had one put aside that he had finished the night before. He started to walk away.

Then he remembered the Christ, "Blessed are the poor in spirit, for theirs is the kingdom of heaven."

He then heard the gruffness of the Roman, "C'mon, Jew, get going. We pay you a lot of money for those death trees. We want it. I have your blood money."

Josiah stopped short. He realized that even the Romans knewthathewasbeinggivenbloodmoneytokillhisownpeople.

The Roman got his cross. Josiah got his silver. He looked inside the bag and once again his stomach turned. It was blood red again. He looked up and saw a beautiful lady standing in front of him. He thought to himself, *Maybe a few hours of entertainment will help.*

He approached her. He took the time to greet her. They started out with small talk that would soon turn to a topic of where he got all of his money.

He realized, at this moment in time, he was not just speaking to a prostitute. He was speaking to a woman who understood who God really was. He brought up the subject of the Christ and her eyes lit up. This woman who Josiah thought he would be able to take advantage of turned out to be a real woman of substance. He looked into her deep brown eyes and saw a fire that burned deeply with a life and hope that he had no idea could be possible. Josiah had to ask one question. Very quickly, he would develop a relationship with this woman who would change his life. He realized she had something he did not. He asked, "Anna, what is it that you have?"

Anna smiled at Josiah. "I really can't put my finger on it. When I spoke to him he reached out and put his hand on my shoulder. I felt a power go through me like I have never felt before in my life. I have a peace that I just cannot understand."

Josiah followed up with another question. "Anna, did that happen when who touched you?"

"The man they call Jesus, silly. The one we have been talking about."

Josiah smiled. "He touched you and all of these great things happened just like that?"

The softness of Anna's voice touched his heart as she said, "The warmth that flowed from his hand through my shoulder was an amazing thing to experience."

Just then they saw the Romans carrying a cross toward the death hill. They saw the chief "freedom fighter" for the Jews being dragged up the hill behind them. Anna got a look of total fear on her face. "That is my brother. He had been leading the freedom fighters against the Romans. They caught him yesterday. I did not know they would be so quick to execute him. My family had been hoping to negotiate his release. He was fighting the Romans as they were taking him up the hill to kill him for trying to destroy a Roman garrison."

Josiah looked over at Anna. She had a tear running down her cheek. He took her hand and pulled her to himself with the hopes of consoling her.

"Who would betray his own people by building those death trees to kill Jews who just want to be free from Roman oppression?" Anna asked with rage in her voice.

The show of emotion caught Josiah totally by surprise. He had no idea how to answer this new person in his life who had given him emotions he had never felt before. He just wanted the question of the death tree to go away. The problem he faced was, he knew the Romans would be back when they wanted to kill another freedom fighter. He thought to himself, *What do I do? If I am honest with Anna, I will lose her. I know that what I am doing is going to be especially hurtful when she finds out I built the cross that they nailed her brother to. She will think I am a person who sells my people for thirty pieces of silver over and over again. The problem is, I am selling my people for thirty pieces of silver. If I lie and she finds out, then I will lose her because she will not be able to trust me! If I show her the crosses, I will lose her.* Josiah made his choice. If it meant losing her, that was a risk he had to take. He would not lie to her. He realized that to lie would just get him found out later and cost any relationship he built with her any way.

"Anna, there is something I need to show you before this goes any further," Josiah said. He took her by the hand and started to lead her to his house to show her his shop.

Anna's eyes glimmered as she responded, "Josiah, let's walk down to the sea first. Jesus is going to be there today and I really want to hear what he has to say."

Josiah nodded and headed to the Sea of Galilee hand in hand with Anna. *At least I can have a few hours of relationship with this beautiful lady. At least I can enjoy this part of my life for a few more hours before my sin destroys it.*

As they arrived, the man they called Jesus the Christ was getting into his boat. He started preaching. He was teaching in Parables.

*   *   *

"A rich land owner was going away to do business. He trusted the men according to their ability. To one he gave five talents, to another three, and to the last one."

Anna and Josiah sat on the grass enjoying each other's company and were entranced by the teachings of the one they called the Christ, they looked into one another's eyes and smiled.

Josiah once again thought to himself. *I have to do one of two things. Either I walk away from the death trees, quit making them, and what the Romans do to me they do, or I tell Anna what I am doing and what happens happens. No! I need to do both. Anna is too important not to. I just pray she can find it in her heart to forgive me.*

Anna looked over at Josiah and simply said, "Josiah, what is wrong? Your face has so much tension in it." She took his hand in hers and gave him a sweet, simple smile. Her eyes had a tenderness about them that melted his heart. Yet at the same time he knew he was doing something that she detested with the innermost parts of her being. He built death trees.

How do I keep her in my life? How do I tell her and not destroy what is building here?

They then heard the Christ say, "Do onto others as you would have them do onto you. For this sums up the Law and the prophets."

Then they heard him say something else, "You cannot serve God and Mammon for you will hate one and serve the other."

It was like the Christ was talking directly to him.

What am I going to do? he thought to himself. *What am I going to do? If I stop, I lose money beyond anything I have ever made or will ever make again. If I keep making these death trees I could be becoming an enemy of God himself. Man, I hate to lose all of this money.*

Just then, Anna took his hand and said, "Josiah, you have something you really want to show me. Take me there now."

Josiah's heart sank. He knew he was about to lose someone who had become very close to him. Here was a beautiful young lady who loved God and loved her people.

She reminded him of the story of Esther. He knew what he had to do. She had to know the truth.

"Let's go," he said. With that, they proceeded to walk to his home. He led her out to the out building where he built the death trees. When Josiah opened the door Anna froze.

Josiah looked at her and saw tears starting to run down her cheeks.

"Josiah! How could you?" Anna said crying. "I could never give myself to the man who kills his own people. I really could not give myself to someone who killed my brother." She turned and ran away from Josiah with a determination never to look back.

Josiah leaned back against the wall and started to cry like a baby. His choice to build the death trees had just cost him the most wonderful woman he had ever met. He walked up to one of the crosses and spit on it. *Why? Why had I decided that it was a good idea to build these death trees?*

3
......
Trapped with No Way to Turn

I t was now the morning of the Sabbath. Josiah knew he had a day off from building the death trees. He felt trapped into something that both destroyed the lives of those nailed to it, but would also destroy everything that he would love to build in his own life.

The death tree had already cost Josiah the one who could have been the love of his life. Sure he could have any woman he wanted, but he would never find one with a heart like Anna. Somehow he understood that the answer was in the Christ. Somehow he had to find him and have just a few moments to discuss how he gets away from the sin that had him chained.

Josiah dressed and walked out into the sunshine. He walked for miles and miles trying to follow where the Christ might be. Then it hit him like a bolt of lightning. It was the Sabbath; he would be at temple. He made his way to Solomon's Temple. He looked at its grandeur and beauty and felt humbled by it all. He saw a crowd gathered and had to see what was going on. He walked up and looked over the shoulder of a smaller person in front of him. He could see the Christ standing beside a man lying on a bed in front of him. He heard the Christ speak.

"Rise."

The man got up, took his bed and started to leave. The Pharisees standing close by became enraged with the Christ. How would he dare heal on the Sabbath? Then he heard the Christ speak. "Who among you if he had an ox fall into a pit on the Sabbath will not pull him out? How much more will our Father in heaven heal a man on the Sabbath?"

The fact that they were being silenced by a son of a carpenter enraged them even more. Josiah's thoughts were going wild at this point. *Jesus better watch* then prayed. *God, please don't let that happen. I could not live with myself.* He prayed as he put the thought out of his mind, realizing he would be the one building Christ' death tree.

He watched the Christ as he walked the streets. He saw him touch people and they would be healed. He wanted to have some time to talk with him. Deep down inside he felt a terror at someday being in the presence of God himself and trying to explain how he could keep building the death trees. He began to realize that he was headed for something that would eventually destroy him eternally. He began to realize that, for him anyway, this life may be all that there would be. God would either utterly destroy him or burn him in hell forever for the destruction he was causing to his own people of Israel. He reached a conclusion. *I may as well get all the pleasures out of this life that I can.* He turned from the Christ just as he was about to talk to him and walked away.

*   *   *

He woke on the first day of the week. He got up, walked out to the sunshine, and looked up into the clear blue sky. His new mindset was that of a man at a point of standing at the edge of a cliff. If he stepped off of it, he would begin to live a life of total depravity. If he turned back, he would choose to live a good and honest life on this earth, thinking there would be no reward for his actions because of the life he had lived on this earth up to that point. His sin was so grievous that there could be no forgiveness for it. He had a vision in his mind. He could see himself on the edge of the cliff. He looked back at a life built without righteousness and could see no reward for it. He made his choice and stepped off the cliff, thinking, *I am going to be condemned for what I have done. So let's just have fun and let the chips fall where they may.*

*   *   *

That afternoon the Romans came to him requesting another cross. He gave them the cross and took the thirty pieces of silver for it. He then proceeded to walk into town looking to go to the Inn to have wine with some of the less than stellar members of the social order. After a couple goblets of the fine wine, he then started to brag about how much money he made with each death tree he created.

"I make more money with one of those in one day than you guys make picking crops for a landowner in a year. I am looking at buying my own property soon."

Soon he found himself surrounded by his fellow countrymen. He would soon discover that even a Jew who was not an upper class member of the Jewish society was still a loyal Jew. He would also soon learn that betraying your own people makes you not only an outcast of those people, but they also see you as a traitor to your own people, and actions that were not pleasant for the traitor would follow. Josiah was about to become a man without a country.

The Romans kept coming to him. He kept building the crosses for thirty pieces of silver for each cross. Time after time he would meet the Christ on the road. Time after time those deep brown eyes of the Christ would cut into his soul. It was like Jesus knew what his destiny was and was willing to accept it.

*   *   *

One morning when he woke to the sound of Romans at his door, he delivered the cross, took the money, and headed for the Inn. He wanted to numb the guilt over what he was doing. As he arrived at the crossroads inn, he was thinking to himself. "*Just get me away from the guilt and pain. I want a clear heart again. I feel like my heart is black. What do I do? How do I get away from this constant feeling that God hates me?*"

*   *   *

When he walked into the inn, everyone at the counter walked away. The innkeeper asked him, "What can I get you?"

Josiah looked inside himself and simply said, "A clear conscience."

The innkeeper looked at Josiah and said, "Josiah, I have known you since you were knee high to a grasshopper. You won't find peace until you repent of what you're doing. Go to the priest and find out what kind of offering you need to make to cover your sin. What you are doing is so evil. You helped kill God's chosen people. He is not going to take that lightly."

Josiah walked out in a daze. His eyes were now glassy as he had just had any hope of redemption wiped from his mind. He saw a young prostitute selling herself on a corner. He would pay her for her services just to escape from his guilt for a few moments. Yet that did not help either.

*   *   *

The next morning, he once again woke to the hopelessness of his situation. The Romans were at his door to buy another death tree and he would sell it to them. With every tree he felt the guilt of betraying his people grow heavier and heavier. He walked down the dirt streets of Jerusalem only to find himself face to face with the Christ. He started to look away, and the Christ drew his vision back to himself. Josiah was about to say something. Jesus smiled and turned and walked away. Jesus looked to heaven knowing exactly what the Father had in mind.

Josiah looked to heaven. He looked this way and that. He felt a deep cry within himself to have conversation with the Christ. Yet it always seemed to escape him. He asked himself, *Why can I not break through? Is my sin so bad that he won't talk to me either?*

Somehow, he felt the love of Christ as the words "Not yet," went through his mind.

"Not yet? Where did those words come from?" Josiah thought to himself as he walked along the dusty road.

The day was getting long and hot, and Josiah really needed to get in some clear fresh water just to get cleaned off. He felt like dirt. He felt unclean from the inside out. He came to the River Jordan, looked around, removed his clothes, and dove in. The cool water over his hot skin felt good. He finished washing and climbed out. Yet, he still felt the filth of his sin.

Josiah looked up and saw the Christ again. He heard him teaching.

"Man does not live by bread alone, but by every word that proceeds from the mouth of God."

Josiah shook his head. He was making money hand over fist, yet he was not happy. He began to ask himself one simple question, but he would find the answer was very complex.

What do I do know? God, what do you want me to do?

He tried to listen but nothing happened. The Christ had walked away and he had no idea where he had gone.

Josiah had questions he needed answers to. There was a panic going on in his mind. *What can I do?*

That night the Romans pounded on his door. Josiah walked to the door and opened it. "What do you need?"

The answer from the centurion was gruff and short. "You know what we want."

Josiah took him to the outbuilding. Josiah felt compelled to ask a question. "What happens if I decide not to build more of these?"

The centurion answered, "That's simple. We nail you to one of these trees."

Josiah turned white with fear. The fear on his face was evident. "So you're telling me there is no end to this job. I quit, I die?"

"Precisely," was the answer that came quickly.

Josiah took the money for the death tree and walked away. His mind was racing. *God, what do I do? I am so sorry I am doing this to your people. What do I do?*

He turned to walk back to his home. There was a boy who looked to be twelve. He had a real gentle look about him.

"Josiah," the young boy said.

Josiah did a double take. "How did you know my name?"

The young boy did not answer. He simply said, "Follow me."

They walked for what seemed like miles. Soon he could see the Christ. He turned to look at the young boy and he was gone. He had an uneasy feeling for what was really going on. Just then he heard it. A scream, and he knew that another freedom fighter was being nailed to a death tree. He reached into his pocket and felt the bag containing thirty pieces of silver. He knew what he had done. The question was, how could he stop?

Still sitting on the rock from the morning, he snapped back to reality. In his mind he had gone over and over what had happened the last several months. He would get up from the rock and go home.

4

. . . . . .

You Are Forgiven

He arose the next morning. Somehow everything felt different. It was like he was about to have a new beginning. Josiah had made up his mind the next time the Romans came to his door he was going to refuse to sell them a cross. But soon his resolve would be put to the test. The knock on the door came. He tried to ignore the knocking, but it just got louder and louder. Soon the knocking stopped. He thought to himself, *Good, maybe they will go to another vendor.* That was not to be the case. He looked out his window and saw the Romans carrying off a cross. Then he heard his door open and a bag of silver dropped on the floor. He shook his head wondering who he had killed that day. He decided he needed something to quiet his soul.

* * *

He walked out into the hot afternoon sun. As he walked along he crossed Anna's path. They stopped within a foot of each other. Their eyes connected and once again they looked into each other's souls.

Anna asked, "Josiah, are you still making and selling the death trees?"

"Yes," came the sheepish answer from Josiah.

Immediately the tears started to run down Anna's cheeks. "How could you keep killing our freedom fighters? You're such a traitor." She turned and stormed away.

Josiah turned and there was the little boy again. "Come with me," the boy said. The little boy led him out into the field where the Christ was teaching.

"The righteous will shine forth as the sun in the kingdom of their Father," Josiah heard the Christ say.

Josiah then thought to himself, *What about me? I am a sinner. How could I shine that bright? There is not any righteousness in me.*

The Christ looked over at Josiah and the Christ with a knowing look on his face smiled. Josiah's eyes met the Christ's once again. The unconditional love that emanated from him started to break the shell that Josiah had put over his life. He turned to look at the boy to ask him a question and he was gone. He looked back at where the Christ was and he was walking away. Josiah felt alone. Then he thought, *I have all this money. I have built twenty crosses. I have six hundred pieces of silver.* He thought of buying land or another donkey. What could he buy to ease his mind about what he was being forced to do now? He looked to the west. He could see the sun was starting to get low in the sky. He knew he had to get home so he could sleep on this. He tried and tried to understand the pain he was causing. He knew the people who loved the men the crosses he was making were giving such a cruel long lasting unmerciful death to.

The guilt flooded Josiah like a tidal wave. He walked around his house shaking his fist in the air. He kept blaming God the Father, the Great I Am, for his failures. He was trying to figure out just how to get out of making the crosses without getting nailed to one himself. Then he thought maybe death is what he deserved for what he had done. He had a battle going on inside his mind and heart. He could not find peace in his soul. He could resign himself to the fate of forever being a traitor, or he could quit and face possibly being nailed to one of the death trees he created himself.

He walked outside into the night air. He looked up into the stars, shaking his fist. He turned and there was that young boy again.

He spoke two words to him, "Your greed."

Josiah felt the anger flush through his body. He turned away so not to take out his frustrations on the boy. When he turned back the boy was gone.

My greed? he thought. *What did he mean my greed?*

He continued to walk in the darkness. Aimlessly he wandered the night. Searching the deepest part of his soul trying to find the reason for continuing to walk. It was almost as if a bolt of lightning hit him in the head.

"I got it!" Josiah said. "The Romans came to the field looking for a stooge to build the death trees. Then my wanting to get out of the field and my greed were the reasons I bought into the whole plan. Now what?"

He walked for hours trying to think of just how he could get out of what he was doing building those damnable death trees. His heart ached at the idea he was sending his own countrymen to their painful, wretched deaths. He shook his head and continued to walk in the dark. He asked himself over and over again, "What do I do now?" His mind was racing. Plan after plan went through his mind. The only problem was that it all seemed to end up in the same place. He could see himself getting nailed to a cross. He had to see Anna. But would she talk to him? There was only one way he could really find out. He made his way to the home of her parents.

*　*　*

Josiah started to walk to the door. Fear of what would happen enveloped him like a cloud. He continued to walk to the door. He knocked with shaking hands. He heard footsteps. He heard the door handle slide to the left. The door opened and Josiah saw a huge man. It was Anna's father.

"What do you want, you murdering traitor?" came the gruff question from Anna's father, Levi.

Josiah could feel the lump in his throat. The fear of this man permeated Josiah's very being. He started to explain, "Levi, I was so..."

"You were wrong! You provided the trees to kill multitudes of our freedom fighters, and one of them was my son, and you were wrong!" Levi screamed at him. "If you ever get close to my daughter again; I will personally see that you never have a child!"

The emotion Levi was showing hit him like a fist in the stomach. Josiah was trying to pound those intense words out of his mind, but he could not. He knew and understood what he had to do. He had to honor Levi's position as Anna's father. He turned and walked away with his head looking down at the dirt beneath his feet.

* * *

Suddenly he heard the gruff voice of the Roman calling him. Josiah tried to ignore it and walked away. The Roman called again, this time in a much more profane manner.

"I need a cross. Are you going to get me one, or do I have to nail you to one?" he shouted.

Josiah's mind was racing. He did not want to be a part of another freedom fighter being nailed to a death tree. However, he did not want to be nailed to one either. The thought went through his mind. *It does not make sense for both of us to die. He dies no matter what.* With that, Josiah took the Roman to the shed and gave him another death tree that he had built weeks before.

* * *

When he stepped out of the shed where the death trees were kept, he just about ran into the little boy. He looked up to Josiah and simply said, "Why are you helping to kill the Father's children? Don't you know God our Father has rewards for those who kill his people and that is one

Josiah blinked and the little boy was gone. He turned to walk away and saw the Christ coming on a colt of a donkey. The people were shouting with an excitement that he had not seen in the past. He thought to himself, *This will not be good.* The thoughts raced through his mind. *Does he not know that no one can openly be praised like he is being praised? He will draw attention to himself. This could put him on a cross as a freedom fighter. He is doing so much good in the world. Why would he risk it?* He turned to walk away.
The little boy was behind him again.

He looked Josiah in the eye and asked one question. "How does it feel knowing that there goes a man of God and He is being led like a lamb to slaughter, and it will be a death tree that you made that kills him?"

Josiah dropped to his knees. He started to sob uncontrollably and curled up in a fetal position. The crying quaked his whole being.

* * *

Josiah looked back on the rock he had been sitting on for the last couple of hours while his mind had been wandering over all the things that had happened over the last couple of months. The sun was starting to descend into the western sky. He knew he had to get back to the tomb. Somehow the wind had changed. There was a sweetness in the air. There was a new excitement that he could not understand. He felt more and more compelled to make his way back to the tomb. But Jesus was dead. Why would he go back there again? Jesus was dead. Josiah felt driven.

For whatever reason he had to return to the tomb one more time and spend one more night.

*   *   *

Twenty minutes later he was at the tomb. One of the centurions asked Josiah, "Were you not the one who built the cross for this man? Why then are you here? Are you also making sure no one steals the body?"

Josiah looked at the men with contempt in his eyes. "This was a good and honorable man and you killed him," Josiah said with an anger that would scare even the bravest soldier.

The big Roman stood up to Josiah. "Listen, Jew. You built the cross for money. We paid you and you built the tree that we hung him out to die on. His blood is on your head." He stared back with absolute disdain.

By this time, it was getting extremely dark. Everyone bedded down for the night. There was however one Roman standing guard at all times. This Roman looked at Josiah and asked, "Weren't you there when I nailed him to the tree?"

Josiah's face shone in the light of the fire. Josiah looked at the Roman. "That was me. I helped kill an innocent man. I don't even know why I am here. He's dead. There is nothing I can do about that."

"I'm Patrous," the Roman said. "Who are you?"

"I am Josiah."

"Josiah, you're a Jew, correct?"

"That's right," Josiah responded, a bit perturbed.

"Word has it, the reason they have us standing guard is there is a prophecy in your writings about the Messiah being nailed to a tree and on the third day walking out of the grave. You being a Jew should know this," Patrous said, looking Josiah directly in the eyes. "They want to make sure no one steals the body until after the third day."

"If that prophecy is true, we will see the world change in short order," Josiah stated hopefully.

This night would prove to be cold and continued to get colder. Josiah was uneasy as there seemed to be a fight going on in the heavens. With all this going on, Josiah still felt complete peace. It was as if he knew the darkest and coldest was just before dawn. He had been there for hours. He had witnessed the coarse jestings of the Romans. He looked to the east and the horizon was starting to get lighter. He looked at the stone in front of the opening to the tomb. It started to roll with no one rolling it. There was a huge flash of white and red light. All the Romans ran in fear, except one. The ground trembled. Josiah watched the Christ rise and walk out of the grave. Josiah shook his head in total disbelief. *How can this be?* he asked himself.

The Christ looked directly at Josiah. Josiah ran to him, dropped to his knees, and tried to kiss his feet. The Christ put out his right nailpierced hand, stepped back and motioned for Josiah to rise.

Josiah began to weep without being able to stop. His crying from deep within was from his very soul. As he was crying, he kept pleading, "Forgive me, please forgive me?" His whole body shook he was crying so hard.

Patrous could not help himself. He too ran to the Christ with tears running down his cheeks as well. He too dropped to his knees with the same pleadings as Josiah.

The Christ looked at the two who were about to hear the only three words the Christ would ever say to them audibly.

"You are forgiven."

As the Christ looked at them, Josiah could feel a power go through him that he had never felt before, but this he would experience over and over again as the Holy Spirit would flood him with power to stand against the very gates of hell. He turned to walk away from the Christ and felt his nail-pierced hand touch his shoulder. He turned and the Christ smiled and said to the two men standing in front of him, once again they heard, "You are forgiven." He nodded as he walked away having pronounced their forgiveness.

Josiah walked back to his home as Patrous started to walk back to his garrison. Then Patrous stopped and turned and walked inside the tomb and thought, *Lord, show me what to do. I don't want to be killing any more people. I want to serve you with all my heart, soul, and mind. Show me what do to.* He then left the tomb and made his way back to the garrison. He walked to his quarters and stood before his bed. He then looked to the heavens knowing that he had just witnessed the world being changed forever. With that he blew out the candles and went to bed.

5

. . . . . .

A New Beginning

Josiah was sound asleep when the bright sun started to shine into his bedchamber. As he looked up, he saw a dove land on his window. Looking into the bird's eyes, it was as if the bird knew him. The black eyes of the dove seemed to be communicating with his spirit. He just did not have a clue what it was trying to communicate. It was as if this bird could see into his soul. It was a spiritual thing that was going on to touch his spirit with God's.

Having gotten up he started to wander the streets. Josiah had purposed in himself while in the presence Christ that his time for him building the death trees was over. From that second on he had one purpose in mind. That purpose was to serve the Father through the Son. He scratched his head and wondered how he would do that. He heard something in back and turned to see what it was. There was that young boy again.

The young boy took his hand and said, "I am taking you to the eleven, they will train you in the ways of the Christ."

With that he led him through the streets of the city. They came to a building. The little boy led him to the upper room. When Josiah walked in, one could hear a pin drop. The instant hatred he felt as he walked into the room shook him to his core.

Josiah looked at all gathered in the upper room. He could only muster two words. "Forgive me."

Peter looked over at him and said, "I denied him, he forgave me. We forgive you. The last thing the Christ told us was to wait in Jerusalem until the Holy Spirit came upon us. If you are willing to stay, you're welcome to join us. I don't know what will happen when the Holy Spirit does come, but it should be interesting."

The next thirty-five days passed quietly. Josiah was hiding from the Romans, as he was not yet ready to deal with them about not making more death trees.

Then on the fortieth day, it happened. Josiah was with the other believers in a quiet place away from everyone who would try put to a stop to what God the Father would do in the upper room. There was a multitude of believers there who were also staying away from the Romans. These believers were from all over. At first he thought he felt a breeze. Then it became like a mighty wind. He looked around and there was a flame above everyone's head. Josiah was totally confused by this whole thing. He could understand what everyone was praying. Everyone could understand what he was praying. But people were there from other countries. It was as if the Tower of Babel had never happened way back when.

He then heard Peter start to speak, explaining the whole thing. At great length Peter explained what the Christ had done by going to the cross that Josiah created. Josiah realized finally that he had a part in man's salvation. That the death tree he created was used to bring him to a point of realizing that it was only through the shed blood of the Christ that he could be saved. He walked over to Peter and asked him what he had to do to be saved. Peter led him in a prayer of repentance and acceptance. He then took him out and baptized him. It was at that second that something changed in him. It was as if God himself had entered his heart and mind. It was at this point he knew he had to go home. It was at this point he knew he had to face the Romans. He went home and went to bed.

* * *

The next morning, he woke. He heard the Romans at the door. They wanted another cross. He laid in his bed and asked God the Father through the Christ what he should do.

Josiah heard the words of the Holy Spirit in his ears. He could not sell them a cross. He realized at that second that this choice could lead to his own physical death. He had seen the risen Christ. He knew in his innermost being that death had been conquered. He had to tell the soldiers what he had seen.

Josiah looked at the lead centurion and said, "I was there when the man they called the Christ walked out of that grave. You were there when he forgave both of us. You can say his body was stolen but we both know it is a lie."

Pointing to another Roman, he said, "As a matter of fact, you were there as well."

The Roman interrupted him. "I was not there." Josiah walked up to him nose to nose and said, "You know you are lying through your teeth. You saw him too. He spoke to you too. The best thing you could do now is drop to your knees and ask God the Father through the Son to forgive your sins and ask Christ to be your lord and savior. You do this and you will feel God himself through his spirit start to indwell your heart."

The Roman first got a real angry look on his face. Then his anger turned softer. Then he looked at Josiah and said, "You're right, I saw him walk out also. I heard him speak to you and me at the tomb. He said we are forgiven, did he not?"

The other Roman would have no part of it. "We are here for a cross!" he barked.

Patrous looked at him and said, "Go to another provider, or better yet, you also should listen to what Josiah has to say, something happened at the tomb. Jesus really did walk out of the grave. We need to listen to Josiah and find out why all this happened."

The lower ranked Roman simply left.

Josiah looked the Roman straight in the eyes and said, "You are forgiven" were the words. You know you remember. Those were the only three words he ever spoke directly to us." He continued. "Those words changed my life. And if you let them they will change yours as well. Then when the Holy Spirit fell on us the power that was and is amazing. My friend, now is not the time to be trying to kill more innocent people who simply want freedom. Now is the time to give your heart to the God of Abraham, Isaac, and Jacob through his only begotten Son Jesus the Christ of Nazareth."

With that Josiah stopped talking. He knew the Holy Spirit had just spoken through him and he had to just stop talking and let the Spirit do his work. He watched the Roman. He could see the Spirit working on him.

He watched his facial expressions. He watched as the tears started to fall. He watched as the God of Abraham, Isaac, and Jacob through the sacrifice of His Son, by His Holy Spirit changed a hard, callous man from the inside out. Josiah understood where this new adventure that started with him making crosses would end up. But on this morning he was about to see the mighty hand of God himself work on a man in a way no human could.

He was seeing a change of heart that would change lives around him and have an impact on people for centuries.

The Roman had a flood of emotions going through his mind. He tried to deny what he saw, but could not. He had seen the risen Christ.

They had tried to pay him to lie, but he knew what he had seen. But the question in his mind was what would he do with what he knew?

Josiah said to him, "Look, if you surrender yourself to the Lordship of Christ and stop trying to figure out things on your own, then and only then you will see the God of Abraham and Isaac and Jacob start to work in your life in ways that will amaze you."

Josiah could tell what the Roman was thinking. His facial expressions kept changing. Josiah knew that his mind must be racing a thousand miles an hour. The Holy Spirit of God nudged him, telling him to say nothing more, but allow the Spirit.

The Roman looked at Josiah. Walked over to him, put his arm on his shoulder, and pulled Josiah to himself and started to cry on his shoulder. Through his sobs, he kept saying, " I have killed so many innocent people, how could God ever forgive me?"

Josiah looked at the Roman and said, "Your sins and mine were the reason he went to the death tree that I created. Your sins and mine were the reasons he was willing to take the excruciating pain of dying the most hateful death known to man. Your sins and mine were the reason he walked out of the grave in the victory over those sins that we could not win."

Before he could say more, the Roman interrupted, "I nailed him to it. I am guiltier than you are. I nailed the Son of God to the death tree. How could he forgive me?"

Josiah could see the pain on the Roman's face. He walked over, put his arm across his shoulders, looked deeply into his eyes, and simply said, "He did, you heard those same three words that I did. 'You are forgiven.' He paid the price, he walked out of the grave. He bought our forgiveness. We have to let go of our sins. To hold it is to say that what he did was not

worth it. Your sin and my sin were paid in full. Walk in that. Let your sin go. It's time for us to go to work and tell the world about what he has done. You have to tell people you were there and you saw him walk out of the tomb."

By this time, the tears were flooding down the cheeks of the Roman. He was crying uncontrollably. The Roman named Patrous looked at Josiah. "I think it's time we start an adventure. Did the Christ not say we are supposed to go into the whole world and preach the Gospel of Him the Christ and baptize them as well?"

Josiah scratched his head. He looked at Patrous and asked one simple question. "How do we do it? How do we go about preaching the Gospel?"

Josiah then took one look at Patrous and a question. "Are you willing to pray and ask the Christ to be your lord and savior? Peter told me when I was with him that the Christ said, he who believes and is baptized shall be saved. I had Peter baptize me. After you pray and ask Christ to be your lord and savior, I will baptize you."

Patrous got a questioning look on his face. "What does baptism do?"

"That is a question I can't really answer either. I just know it was a command of Christ. I think that's where the Father formally puts His Hand on us."

Patrous smiled and said, "If Jesus said we should do it, that's what I will do."

Josiah responded "We have one big thing that Jesus said to do before he went to the Father. That was to go into the world and preach. That's the major thing we have to do."

Patrous simply said four little words. "We just do it." He continued, "Did not the Christ say not to worry about what we will say? We are all given gifts to use. We need to use those gifts that the Lord will use to create situations for us. Then we just open our mouths and tell of the great works he has and will do."

Josiah looked at Patrous and said, "I think we head for Damascus."

"Why Damascus?"

" I feel like there is something great about to happen. Something is going to happen on that road that will start some amazing changes,"Josiah answered.

The Roman nodded his head in agreement and they headed off.

6
. . . . . .

On the Road to Damascus

The two men were headed for Damascus having no
clue what they were going to be walking into. The
road was dusty, and the smell of camel dung permeated
the air. As they were walking, the people to share their
newfound friendship with the Father through Jesus with
were few. They had one thing in common that drove them.
They had both seen the risen Christ and had a burning
in their hearts to share this information with the rest of
world. The problem they both knew they had was the
simple yet profound truth that could be expressed quite
simply. They had no idea just what they were going to do.
But they knew the world had to know what they had seen.

After they had walked for miles, they saw something
that would have a huge impact on them for years. Up
ahead was a man by the name of Saul. He had been trying
to destroy the church before it even could get started. He
was one of the Pharisees that would not lose his power to
a group of radicals who knew nothing. Josiah and Patrius
had decided to stay way back from him. Suddenly there

was a huge white light enveloping Saul. And a voice could be heard coming from the light that was all over Saul.

"Saul, Saul, why do you persecute me?"

The two men looked at each other. They realized just who was doing the talking. The two men could see Saul shaking his head. Saul fell to his knees inside the light. It almost seemed like there was a whirlwind going on inside the light as the words kept being poured into Saul. Then it happened. Saul was told his name would now be Paul.

The voice came through loud and clear so everyone could hear it.

"Paul, you will be led into the home of Ananias."

At that point both men knew that it was the Lord Jesus talking. Both men knew that Paul was a very learned man and could teach them much about the prophecies about the Messiah. They felt like blank slates. They knew and understood what they had seen, but of the whys and where's they had not a clue. What they did know was that they had a lot to learn.

As quick as the light had come it was gone. It had vanished in the day. The wind was now blowing the dust around. Saul, now Paul, was standing there in the dark. He had been blinded by the Light of Life. He would be blind for three days. The two men followed with the rest of Paul's followers to see what would happen. Josiah and Patrius were hungry to learn of the prophesies that foretold the story of the Christ.

They followed at a distance, not clearly understanding what God the Father had just accomplished using his Son, but they knew it was something, and they knew it would be big. They understood this guy who had been an enemy of what God had been trying to do was now an ally. You see, as Saul he had thought he was doing what God wanted with his intense legalism. One quick encounter with the risen Christ was all it took to show him who the loving Father through the Son by the Spirit really was. They had seen the Risen Christ. Christ had spoken to Josiah, but there were still questions as to why it all happened. They both understood one thing. They understood they had to find out why Jesus had died and rose again. They knew the person with the answer was Paul. They just needed to have a few moments to sit down with Paul so he could explain the prophecies to them. The one thing they did understand was that he for the time being was blind. The men who were with him had to take him to Ananias.

*   *   *

Now Ananias was a prophet. Both men looked at him and decided they had to talk to him before Paul got there. They rushed on ahead as Paul, being blind, was not moving real fast. When they found Ananias they decided to ask him some questions about the Christ. They walked into the temple to talk to the elderly prophet. They mentioned his name and got a curt answer.

"Paul's coming, The Lord our God has words he has instructed me to say to him. I know this, the Lord God has chosen him for an important task, nothing can stand in the way of the task that has been laid out before him," the old prophet told them.

They asked the old prophet one question. "Why did the Christ have to die and walk out of the grave?"

Ananias looked at them and said, "It all started thousands of years ago at the beginning with Adam and Eve."

Like most people of their time, Josiah had heard of Adam and Eve, but had not paid close attention. Patrous had not even heard the names of Adam and Eve and really had no idea what it all meant but would become enlightened. This all would cause his view of the world to be changed.

All the two men could do was to look at each other.

"Whatever project God, through his Son Jesus was working on, must be of great importance. It's like the price has been paid. Neither one of us knew exactly what that meant. But I am sure Paul will be able to fill us in on everything," Josiah said. "I was at Pentecost. I saw men from all over speaking in everybody else's language. I heard Peter speak of people being saved and filled with the Holy Spirit. I know I saw the Christ die. I saw the Christ walk out of the grave. But what I need to understand is why did the Christ do it? Why did he die for our sins?"

Again the two men looked at one another. They began to realize the importance of taking the time to understand what Paul would shortly be teaching them. The two men continued to follow Paul. They knew that he was a teacher of the law. But they had to understand not just that Christ was the fulfillment of the law. They knew that in their hearts. But they had to know why God the Father gave the law. What would be the purpose of a bunch of rules that no one could follow. They knew they would have to follow Paul to gain this knowledge. They knew it was his intellect and knowledge of the scripture they needed to come to an understanding of that would allow them to be totally comfortable explaining the whole picture of what they had witnessed at the cross and at the tomb.

Josiah and Patrous came to the conclusion they had to follow Paul diligently for a period of time to be able to grasp the magnitude of what they had witnessed. They had come to understand that anyone could spout off that Christ had risen from the dead. But to understand the why of why it happened would be what truly would change a person's life forever.

7
......
First Stop, Philippi

I t's here that Paul would start to share the history of the
Jews. Men of faith, Abraham, Isaac, and Jacob would be
explained as historical example of the Fathers of the
Jews. He would share his knowledge of Isaiah in describing
the prophecies about the Christ. How he would deliver
man from his sinful nature. He would even take them back
and explain the fall of Adam and Eve and their putting
man in the situation that he was now in. They came to
realize that man had placed a black spot in every heart
born. The only way to clear man of the blackness in his
heart was by a sacrifice only God the Father could make.
God made that sacrifice by being willing to see his own
Son Jesus The Christ die
and shed his blood for all mankind, so man could be made
holy, and being made holy could once again walk into the
presence of the Father of all mankind who could have
nothing unholy in his presence. He also purposed it in
His mind to raise him from the dead on the third day to
demonstrate His absolute power.

The men, Josiah and Patrous, would start out on their journey from Perga. They felt at this time they had an understanding of why God the Father had sent his Son to purify man so his Spirit could once again dwell within mankind. They walked out of the house that Paul had been staying in and realized in a second two things. One, how small the world was in relationship to the rest of the universe and how big it was in relationship to them. They would stand looking at what was laid out in front of them, and they looked up to heaven and prayed.

"Father, give us the people to talk to. Please send us where you want us to go and do the things you want us to do to reach the people you want reached. In the name of Christ Jesus, Amen."

With that they headed out on an adventure that would lead them to the victories that the Father had planned.

The two were just starting to wake up the next morning. Their heads were still foggy from a very sound sleep. They looked up and saw Paul staring down at them. He looked at the men and simply told them, "We are heading next to Philippi. What I want you to do is go to Ephesus and start getting things set up for me there."

Josiah had one question. "What is it you want us to do when we get there?"

Paul looked at them and chuckled. "I want you to start to talk to them about Jesus the Christ, his crucifixion and his resurrection. You two were at both. You have a testimony most people just don't have. Our Father, the great I Am, allowed you to see both the defeat then the following conquest of death and sin by his Son. It's time to get up and get to work. We have been placed here for such a time as this, and it is time to get to work." He took the men aside to tell them just to listen to what the Spirit that came down at Pentecost would communicate to them, and use what the Spirit of God himself would do to lead the people to them that God the Father wanted them to speak to. The people the Holy Spirit would be bringing them in contact with needed the salvation that only the Christ could give them. Their testimony would be needed to convince them of who Jesus really is.

The leaders of the temple were getting really nervous because there was no physical body of Christ. They realize that their "kingdom" was about to fall down around them. They would do anything to stop that from happening.

Early the next morning, Josiah and Patrous sat together eating a breakfast of grapes, bread, and water. They ate in silence knowing the journey that lay ahead of them would be one of adventure, pain, and hardship. They also understood that the journey that was before them was so important because the eternity of many men women and children, not just now, but for hundreds of years to come, depended on them following through on the gift that the Father had given them through the Son. They had a story to tell. It was the true story of what they had seen with their own eyes. Paul was taking the time to educate them on why what happened was the key to understanding what they had really seen at the tomb.

They packed their donkeys and headed for Ephesus. The figured out they had a couple hundred miles of pack ing to get to their destination. They looked at each other, nodded, and started the journey of a lifetime.

Their path would be to follow the coastline of the Mediterranean Sea. Walking the coastline, they would find the same thing over and over again. They kept finding people searching for meaning to their lonely, depraved lives. People who had experienced everything this carnal life could give. Physical experience after physical experience netted them the same thing. In one word: emptiness. People had begun asking themselves one question. Why am I here? What is the meaning to this whole existence? Both men would look at each other and know one thing. Christ was the answer to all the emptiness. From his teachings, to his death on the cross and his walking out of the grave, the meaning to this life was revealed. He opened the door to the Holy Spirit of God to dwell not in places made by man's hands, but in men's hearts.

What they were to find out was that two forces would be used against them to try to stop that which Christ had accomplished on the Cross. One was the Jewish leaders, and the other would be the Roman government who did not want some other "king" invading their space. What they were to find out was that Romans liked to destroy anything that drew people to the Messiah as they were afraid Christ's kingdom was on the earth.

The road along the sea was more than a little dusty. Josiah and Patrous were more than a little thirsty. The wind coming off the sea was driving the dust, making talking to each other difficult. The men would not be deterred from the purpose set before them. They had seen the Christ walk out of the grave and they would start spreading the word that would have an eternal effect on men's souls. They knew and understood that God had accomplished something in sending his son that man himself would never have been able to do. That was to be a sacrifice of such a high nature that it would not just cover man's sin, but completely cleanse a man of it.

As they walked the windy seaside, they spotted a caravan of camels and donkeys being led by what seemed to be servants of royals coming toward them. As they looked closer it seemed to be leaders of the temple. As they got closer and closer they started to realize that the men coming toward them really were the leaders of the temple.

As they got closer and closer, Josiah said to Patrous, "We need to pray. Our Father is leading these leaders of his temple to us for one reason. That reason is for us to talk to them. But it has to be done right or we may cause more problems for ourselves."

Then Patrous answered, "We must remember this important truth. Perfect love cast out all Fear. What the Christ did and we witnessed was perfect love. We saw him die, and we saw him walk out of the grave. We have to be able to communicate that."

With that the men joined in prayer for the words to come from the Father himself through them by his Holy Spirit.

As the men approached they recognized Josiah. "Aren't you the one who made the cross that they nailed that lunatic Jesus to?" they asked in a tone of hatred toward the Christ.

The leader continued, "I hope you men don't buy into the 'raised from the dead' lie. You do understand that they stole the body, don't you?"

Patrous, being a man who hated lies more than anything, gave a little chuckle as he said, "You men are supposed to be the leaders of the Jews. The people depend on you for truth and honesty. God himself is your judge concerning the way you lead his people. Now if God really did send his Messiah, how would you handle it? Would you welcome him, or would you nail him to a cross?"

The leader got a real indignant look on his face. The question he had for Patrous was immediate. "Where you there when they nailed him to the death tree?"

Josiah answered that one. "As a matter of fact, I was. It was the only time with all the crosses I built that I had to see what happened." He continued, "I was also there on the third day, as was my friend here. We saw the Christ walk out of the grave."

At first the leaders of the temple froze. Then the look that came over the faces of the leader was one of anger and disgust. "How dare you speak that way. He made himself equal to God. To give that false testimony is stoneable."

The answer Josiah gave was quick and with even more intensity. "How dare you break the law by accusing us of lying? You know that you paid off the soldiers to keep quiet. My friend here cannot be bought."

Patrous got a sly grin on his face as he said, "How much are you willing to pay for me to be quiet about this?"

The answer came just as quick. "Thirty pieces of silver for you and your friend if you just forget what you saw."

Patrous responded, "You mean to tell me that you will pay me not to say exactly what I saw at the tomb? Yet you told us it never happened. We saw it, we know what we saw. You're so afraid of losing your power over people you will try to buy their eternity for thirty pieces of silver. Just how corrupt are you anyway?"

The anger in the eyes of the leaders was clear. As they walked away they warned both Patrous and Josiah. "You better watch it. Your days on this earth are numbered."

The two men looked at each other and said three words at the same time: "Be not afraid."

Then they both grinned as Josiah said to the priests walking away, "Remember what Solomon wrote. It is appointed for man once to die and then the judgment. We are not scared of our judgment. But Christ himself said it would be better for a millstone to be tied around one's neck than to cause one of his little ones to stumble. You are causing a lot of God's kids to stumble. I would be more worried about what is going to happen after you die than we need be."

From that time on they knew they were going to be watched very closely as the Jewish leaders had one thing on their mind, stomping out anyone who would talk of

Christ, especially the eyewitnesses. *   *   *

As the two men arrived in Philippi, they were taken in by the beauty of the city. The people walked around doing business just as they had been doing for centuries before. The two men knew and understood the people really had no idea why they were there, they just knew they had daily tasks to perform to be able to live the life they had been placed in for whatever reason they had been placed on this earth.

Some people had been born into wealth, and some people had been born into poverty. The people with wealth took advantage of the people of poverty to make themselves more wealthy. What they did not realize was that it did not matter what station in life they were born into. The Heavenly Father of Abraham, Isaac, and Jacob sent his Son the Christ so that their ultimate end would no longer be the grave, or worse, but would be an eternity with the Father through the Son by the Spirit.

The two men understood why Paul had sent them ahead of his arrival in Philippi. There was a lot of work that had to be done before he arrived in the town to start to teach these people about the Christ and what he had done and why he did it. They also knew and understood that both the Romans and Jews would stop at nothing to see the work of Christ stopped cold in its tracks.

The two men found themselves in the local inn eating. They sat at a table, bowed their heads, and asked the Father through the Son by the Spirit what they should do to prepare the way for Paul who was coming after them. They finished their meal of fish and bread, said good night to those at the inn, and headed off to their tents.

The next morning, as Josiah walked out of his tent into the bright sun shining down on Philippi he saw a familiar face. It was his sweet Anna. He took her face in his hands and kissed her forehead and asked, "Did you walk this far by yourself?"

Anna smiled and stated, "My father had to come here. He said he had to help get things set up for Paul. So I asked him if I could walk with him and see if there was anything I could do to help."

Josiah smiled, thinking he knew the real reason she decided to travel with her father. "The real reason you came along was to see me, was it not?" he asked her with a small grin on his face.

Anna started to get angry again. "It is not!" she said. "I would never in my life have wanted to travel that far to see the person who built death trees to kill his fellow Jews and my brother and make money doing it!" She turned and ran from him in total disgust.

Josiah stood for a second stunned, turned, started to walk away thinking he would never see Anna again. Anger once again permeated his whole being. He stopped and turned to Anna's direction. "Anna, I was there when the Christ walked out of the tomb. I was there when they nailed him to the cross. When he walked out of the grave he said three words to me. 'You are forgiven.' If the Christ forgave me, can't you?"

Anna stopped and looked at Josiah. Tears were running down from her deep brown eyes. All she did was shake her head slightly and turned and walked away.

* * *

This time the anger was within himself as he thought, *"How could I have been so stupid? How could I have ever thought that even though the Christ had forgiven me for what I had done, how could I think that she ever could?"* He realized the tiredness of his soul. He realized as the sun started to disappear behind the hills and darkness started to envelope the country, that his need for sleep would take over and he had to get to the inn where he was staying. The darkness of the night was gaining and forcing the light to disappear by the minute as he walked into the inn and proceeded to his sleeping area. He laid down and sleep took him.

The next day would be spent talking to people. He would tell them what he and Patrous had seen: The Christ walking out of the grave. Josiah would admit he was the one who made the cross of Christ. But then the question came. "Why did the Christ have to come and die and walk out of the grave?"

Josiah and Patrous told them that Paul would clear that part up. They explained that Paul was much bet-ter versed on the ins and outs of prophecy than they were. The only thing they knew was both men had had a hand in killing the Christ and both men had seen him walk out of the grave. And both men were forgiven by the Christ immediately when he walked out of the grave and Paul would explain all of the reasons for it.

Having spent a few days talking to many people they really felt an unction of the Holy Spirit to head for Antioch.

8
· · · · · ·
Antioch

J osiah and Patrous were sleeping soundly. As they woke they found themselves looking directly into Paul's eyes. "Gentlemen," Paul stated with great authority. "The job you have done here getting things set up is above reproach and now it's time for you to move on and start getting things set up in Antioch."

Josiah and Patrous would soon find out that Paul wanted them to travel to Turkey and the city of Antioch to set things up there. They both understood one thing, they had seen the Christ walk out of the grave. They had both heard him pronounce their forgiveness. And they had both felt the instant joy of being cleansed from all of their sin.

Paul also wanted them crossing the Mediterranean Sea to Crete to set things up there as well. They were happy to do so. They could not hide the joy that would go along with them as they told soul after soul about having a part in the crucifixion of the Christ and seeing him walk out of the tomb. And of course, hearing those priceless words spoken to them by the Savior of the world: "You are forgiven."

The more people they would share this with, the more people they would witness drop to their knees and surrender to the lordship of Jesus the Christ. As people were baptized into Christ after their profession of faith, the change happened almost instantly. Things were exciting and were about to get even more so.

*   *   *

As they boarded the ship for Antioch, thoughts of Anna kept going through Josiah's mind. His thoughts went to something he had heard Paul teach. "*Old things are passed away; all things are new. We are a new creation in Christ.* His thoughts continued, *If I have been forgiven by my Father in heaven through The Son by The Spirit why can Anna not find it in her heart to forgive me?*" It was at that second he felt the assurance that Anna too would be able to forgive him in time.

As they crossed the sea, Josiah's mind went over many things. First and foremost his mind went over and over again what he had seen that first morning at the tomb. He kept hearing the voice of the Christ say to him, "You're forgiven." Then his mind would go to the last time he saw Anna and the absolute rejection of him because of his past destruction of her Jewish brothers, as well as her real brother. He could still see the anger in her eyes just before she turned and walked away. Then his mind would go back to the words of the Christ: "You are forgiven."

The thoughts kept going through his mind. *"How is it that I have confidence that at some point Anna will forgive me, but my question is this. At what point?"*

Patrous walked up to him as he leaned on the gunwale of the ship. "My friend, what are you thinking about so deeply?" Josiah really did not want to deal with the question, at the time with anyone else.

"Forgiveness" was the only answer that Josiah would give his friend.

"Forgiveness? We do have a lot to be thankful for. We have both been forgiven of so much," Patrous stated with total gratitude in his voice.

"I know we have been forgiven by what Jesus the Christ did. We have been forgiven by Christ himself, for what we did to him, by his conquest over death and his walking out of the grave. I heard the words 'You are forgiven.' We both heard him speak to us when he walked out of the tomb. But Anna, I thought I heard the voice of Jesus, or the Father, or maybe an angel, tell me she would eventually forgive me. But my question is when is eventually going to happen? Today, tomorrow, next year? When?"

Patrous put his arm round Josiah's shoulder. "My friend and brother in Christ, you have done a lot of damage. I would guess you probably built the death trees that some of her friends died on. Those things are not easily forgotten, and forgiving would be harder yet to do. In the Father's time it will happen."

Josiah stepped away from the gunwale of the ship, looked over at Patrous, and said, "Let's go, no more time for a pity party. We know what we have to do.

People's eternities depend on us following through on what the Christ told us to do. Go into the world and make disciples. We don't have a choice. What happens in this life is a flash in the bucket. Eternity is a long time to be away from The Father."

Josiah turned and walked to the stern of the ship. He could hear the sails flapping in the wind and the water rushing by as he looked up into the blue sky and could almost feel the Father smiling down on him. He could almost hear the spirit say to him, "Josiah, you got it, you really got it. Now you can be used." Having found a hammock, he crawled into it. The gentle rocking of the ship as it cut through the water soon put him to sleep.

Patrous saw an empty bucket sitting on the deck with a rope for dropping it into the sea and filled it with water. One could almost see his brain working as he thought about filling the bucket with water and throwing it on Josiah, just to add some levity to the task that the Father in heaven through his Son Jesus by His Holy Spirit had set before them to accomplish. He knew and understood that Josiah was exhausted. He also understood that soaking him with the water would be so funny. He lowered the bucket into the water, filled it to the rim then walked over to where Josiah was sound asleep. Woosh! Josiah found himself soaking wet and laying on the deck as the force of the water had washed him off of his hammock. Lying on the deck of the ship, his anger started to well up inside him. Then he looked at Patrous standing there with the bucket with a big smirk on his face and he started to chuckle. Then the chuckling turned to laughter.

Soon both men were rolling on the deck with uncontrollable laughter.

Suddenly they heard the familiar call, "Land ho!" The men knew they were coming into Antioch. They both at the same moment said in unison, "Let's pray." They realized the enormity of the task before them. Antioch was not a small town. How would they reach so many people with the good news of what Christ had done? They decided that they would just be themselves. They would start by just talking about what they had seen. They would testify that they had a part in killing the Christ. They would also testify that they had seen the risen Christ walk out of the grave. They would follow that by telling anyone and everyone they come in contact with that the three words the Christ had said to them were "You are forgiven."

*   *   *

As their ship approached the docking area, Josiah looked over at Patrous and said, "Paul told us that Antioch will be the center of his ministry. He wants to use it to reach other key cities in the area with the message of the Risen Christ. We have a lot of work to accomplish. I don't know about you, but I am not an educated man like Paul. But I do know this. I saw Christ die, and I saw him walk out of the grave. I built the death tree, and you nailed him to it. His only words to us when we saw him walk out were 'You are forgiven.' My friend, that's the story that Christ will use to bring people to him. Paul can educate them but our story will be used to save them. We must all work together to spread the truth that Christ is really risen."

Patrous then stated, "Speaking of work, what do you say we get busy and start unloading all of our gear from this ship and get it up on the dock?"

The answer from Josiah was quick. "Let's get busy, bro." It took an hour to unload their gear, they had brought with them. Tents for sleeping in the desert, and a few extra tunics to protect from the hot sun. When all of their gear was safely off the ship, they spent the next couple of hours looking for an inn to spend the night. Finding nothing, they went outside the city and set up camp on the outskirts of town. For the next few weeks before Paul's arrival, they would be talking to people wherever they saw them. They would map out where Paul would be speaking. Having everything ready, they would soon learn that Paul had more in mind for them than being simply his setup men.

As the two men woke and stepped out of their tent, they saw a familiar face. It was Paul.

Paul said. "Gentlemen, you are two who have seen and spoken to the Risen Christ. When I met him on the road to Damascus, I spoke to him when he was in a burning bush. Yet you were close enough to touch his physical risen body and according to what I have heard of your testimony he actually put his nail-pierced hands on your shoulders and pulled you up from your knees at his feet. Your testimony is extremely powerful. Our Father has finished a work he started in the Garden of Eden by his pure and holy sacrifice. I want to have you two as a key part of what we are doing here. Are you willing to help?"

Josiah and Patrous looked at each other and shook the sleep out of their heads. They nodded and in unison said, "Let's get to work." They both realized that because of their experience seeing the Christ, they had been given a unique opportunity to be a part of what Christ was going to be doing in the hearts and minds of men, women, and children for years to come.

As the three of them sat around the morning breakfast fire, cooking their fish, they were also in deep prayer. They realized that the task before them was daunting, but knew they had to touch the heart of the Father at the same time he would touch theirs. They also realized that truth they would be sharing would be grasped with excitement by some and totally rejected by others.

After breakfast they left their camp to go and explore Antioch. As Josiah walked down the street he saw a very familiar face. It was Anna. He walked up to her just to say hello. Anna took one look at Josiah and turned and walked away without a word. Josiah looked to heaven as if to say, "Father, where's the forgiveness? I thought your spirit told me she would forgive me." He would in time find out his time was not necessarily the Father's time.

As Josiah walked along the street he could hear the quiet voice say to him, "Josiah, when the time is right she will forgive you. Trust me."

Josiah then noticed some men with their camels. He walked up to them not knowing exactly what to say to them but trusted Christ enough just to start talking.

They appeared to be men of some wealth, crowns upon their heads and camels that were adorned like noth ing he had seen before. Josiah walked up to the camel and said.

"Sir, may the blessing of the Lord be on you this day."

The royal looking guy on the camel looked down and nodded at Josiah. He saw Josiah was dressed as a Jew. He asked him what brought him to the land of Antioch.

Josiah realized this was a door that the Most High had opened, so he began sharing what he had seen at the crucifixion of the Christ. He spoke at length of how he came to meet the Christ at his resurrection and the words he spoke to him then. The only three words the Christ ever spoke directly to him were: "You are forgiven." He then spoke of the new freedom, and how the Holy Spirit of God himself was living in him.

The look on the nobleman was one of question, excitement, and wonder. He asked a question, "How do I get this freedom?"

With a slight smile, he looked at his new friend and soon-to-be brother. "You simply ask" was all the answer Josiah needed to give. He then asked if he could pray with him. The nobleman agreed to pray. After he surrendered to the lordship of Christ, he then looked over at the sea they were standing beside.

"Baptize me, please?" The nobleman asked.

Josiah then took him down to the sea and baptized him in the name of the Father and of the Son and of the Holy Spirit. He stood on the shore and watched him get back on his camel. He watched him ride off. As he turned there was Patrous standing beside him asking what had just happened.

Josiah smiled. Patrous looked on as Josiah took the time to talk to the men and women about what he and Patrous had witnessed. At the same time Josiah could see the men what looked like priests on the hill beside where he was teaching of what he saw. They looked angry. He thought to himself, "*This could be trouble.*" He looked at Patrous, gave a slight nod in the direction of the priests, and said, "I wonder what they are so angry about."

The priests stormed up to Josiah. "How dare you lie to these people and tell them that the Christ rose from the dead? We have statements from the Romans that his body was stolen."

Patrous walked up to the priest. "Look at me. You're the one lying here. I was there, they tried to bribe me. Offered me thirty pieces of silver to keep my mouth shut. I know what I saw and know this, my testimony cannot be bought."

With a scowl on his face, the priest said, "You guys better watch it. You could end up with the same fate as that Jesus of Nazareth."

The answer Josiah gave the priest totally caught him off guard. "You mean walking out of the grave, being taken up to heaven in a cloud? You're right, that would be a totally amazing experience."

At that point the priest's face was getting redder and redder. The anger this man had toward Josiah and Patrous was a scary thing to watch. "I will see you nailed to one of those death trees, mark my words!," he shouted into Josiah's face. "You cannot blaspheme as you are and not pay the price for it!"

Josiah looked into the face of the Priest and said, "I know what I saw, Christ is risen, and you have no power over me." He turned and walked away from the priest.

As he walked away, the priest was yelling at him angered beyond belief. He was kicking dirt in his direction. Josiah kept walking with Patrous at his side. As they headed downtown, they saw some people coming their way. Patrous looked at Josiah and asked, "Is that not Paul and Silas?"

Josiah walked up to Paul and Silas. He greeted them with a hug, then proceeded to say, "Paul, I am telling the people about what we saw that day when the Christ walked out of the grave. I know man sins and is unclean. But what I don't understand is why did the Christ have to die and walk out of the grave. Can you explain that to me?"

Paul smiled and said, "I am glad you asked me that. You see, it started back when man first chose, in their arrogance, to do that which Father commanded them not to. When man chose to disobey Our Father in heaven, it made mankind unholy and not able to be in our Father's presence any longer. When that happened, Our Father had no choice but to send him out of Eden. From that point in time, Father had started putting things in motion for his Son to be born. He started the events that would lead to the right people being in power at the right time. Father had to have everything lined up so when he sent His Son Jesus everything would click. The Father had to get his message of the coming Messiah through the prophets so the people would be looking for Him. The great I Am understood that the power hungry priests in his temple would reject the Christ. That's why he tore the curtain in the temple. He had a place in the temple for his presence for thousands of years. When they rejected His Son they rejected him. He left the temple. You see the Christ prayed shortly before he was nailed to the Cross that as The Father was in him that he would be in us also. And because they are in us that we would be able to spread His message throughout the world."

Josiah had two emotions coursing through his veins. One was excitement, the other was amazement. He looked at his friend and compatriot Patrous who was having the same emotions. "Now I understand just how important Father's creation is to him. We are his creation, we are the sheep of his pasture, as David wrote. He wants all of his people to come through his son Jesus the Christ. We have been given that message and have to find a way of communicating it to the people," Josiah said.

Paul continued, "Jesus just before his ascension to Heaven gave the command that we should go into all the world proclaiming the gospel of the Kingdom. Baptizing in the name of the Father and The Son and The Holy Spirit. We have a mission. Josiah, you built the cross they nailed Christ to. I persecuted the church. We have both been forgiven."

Patrous looked at Josiah and smiled. "We know when we tell people we saw the Christ walk out of the grave we can add this little statement. When he walked out he completed mankind's redemption. Now when they ask why do they need redeeming, we can tell them now that it has been explained to us. This is so great! I can hardly wait to start talking to people." Patrous then turned and started to walk up to the first person he saw. He started to tell them what he saw. He used the term, "He finished the redemption of man." When the people would ask them, he would explain what the prophets had said. He would explain man's fall in the garden. And he would explain the last words Christ said on the cross: "It is finished." It all made so much sense to him. Patrous and Josiah were starting to see more and more people turn to Christ. They were starting to see more and more people follow Christ in baptism. More and more the priests of the temple were allowing their anger to get hotter and hotter. The more people who were set free caused the priests of the temple to become angrier and angrier. They could see their control over the people slipping away. They knew their form of godliness was without power. They also knew the only power they had was to use God as an anvil to keep the people under their thumb. By their use of the Law that God the Father had intended to be used to show just how much they needed him, and his forgiveness in a way that actually had God the Father not as thee God of love, but as a God of retribution. They were able to control the people's every move. By doing that the people of God were kept from understanding that he was and is full of love and caring as well as justice. It was because of his justice that he had to pay for the sins of the people himself in the person of his Son Jesus Christ who would die for the sins of all mankind. By dying for mankind, he was cleansing mankind so they could once again walk into his presence.

The priesthood thought that by mankind being able to walk into God's presence as purified children of God the Father through the Son by the Holy Spirit they would not be needed anymore, and have to give up their power over God's people.

Paul would share with the people the prophecies that the Christ had fulfilled and how God the Father had used his only begotten Son to deliver man from man's sinful nature. Because of Paul's knowledge of the Holy Writings, they could not refute him. So they would slink off into their holes to plot a way of putting Paul in jail and eventually having him put to death. What they did not realize was by putting Paul in prison they would be increasing his influence tenfold. Paul would write, "What Satan meant for evil, God the Father would use for good."

By this time both Josiah and Patrous had been working hard with Paul and Silas to get the local church working well in Antioch. The people had had their hearts touched in ways that would actually put a fire in them to draw them nearer and nearer to their Father in Heaven through the Son Jesus the Christ. As more and more people were drawn to the Father through the Son, those people would draw more people to the Christ. It was multiplying quickly. The more people started to meet God the Father through his Son the Christ the more the Pharisees and Sadducees saw their grip and control of the people get ripped out of their hands and they saw the people realizing Jesus really was the Messiah and to find true happiness they would have have to surrender their lives to his lordship. They began to realize that the rituals they had been using to cover their sins, were no longer of use, as the ultimate price for their forgiveness had been paid making God's people clean, thus making them whiter than snow, and able to walk into the Father's presence because of the sacrifice the Son made.

Paul decided that he and Silas needed to take Josiah and Patrous aside and spend some time educating them on the importance of blood in the Jewish ritual of purification. They would also spend time showing the importance of coming to the Lord's table to receive communion with Him. They also knew that they had to instruct them in the importance of taking communion in a worthy manner. They taught them that if anyone had a conflict with another believer, they had to resolve that issue before they could come to the table. They had to, as far as they could, clear everything up so they could present themselves truly as a living sacrifice. Paul looked to Silas. He then looked over at Josiah and Patrous and said, "I think it's time we sent you to Peter. Peter spent three years with the Christ during his time on this earth. You have much to learn from him on your journey to be used in the fullest way possible."

9
· · · · · ·

Time with Matthew and Peter

Leaving Paul and Silas, they headed back to Jerusalem to meet with Peter and John to learn more about

the Christ and to assist in any way possible in their ministry. Just about the second they walked into town, Josiah looked up and saw the one who caught his heart two years before. He saw Anna. She smiled at Josiah and his heart melted. The thoughts came flooding back into his mind and he began to wonder. *"Has she forgiven me for the evil that I have done. Or is this going to take even longer?"* Josiah would soon find out.

He walked up to the beautiful Anna. He touched her shoulder and said, "Can we talk?"

Anna smiled as she said, "Sure, what do you have in mind?"

At this Josiah started stumbling for words. The words just would not come. No matter how hard he tried he could not get his mouth to work. He felt like a young boy trying to talk to the cutest girl in class for the first time. He had had totally open conversations with her, yet at this critical time he could not bring himself even to open his mouth to ask for the forgiveness that he so desperately needed. His heart was screaming for him to say something, anything. Yet his mind was telling him to turn and walk away. He knew the Christ had forgiven him, yet the one who he wanted to draw close to on this earth stood there with those big brown eyes looking into his soul waiting for a word, any word, something. Josiah shook his head and turned and walked away.

Anna got a look on her face of total disbelief. She turned and stormed off, convinced that he was not interested in hearing what she had to say. Deep down inside of her she had a sense that he just did not listen to what the Holy Spirit was saying to him. She had an aching in her heart to share with him about what she knew about the Christ. Somehow, someway, she knew she had to talk to him. She had something to say to him and her heart would not rest until she had a chance to tell him. With that she turned and walked in the opposite direction.

Josiah walked up to Peter. Peter looked at him knowing that he had built the Cross that they had used to crucify the Christ. He asked one simple question. "You saw my Lord first when he walked out of the tomb. All the times we talked I never asked you. What did you see when Jesus came back to life. I had seen him raise the dead a few times. Yet I cannot quite imagine the energy that would have been there when He came back to life. What happened in that moment in time?"

"I did all the teaching. I know what you experienced was amazing. I just never really got a chance to fully understand what you saw, and what the Christ actually told you."

Josiah smiled and answered, "That is true. There was a flash that came from behind the stone. It rolled on its own, it seemed like. Then Jesus the Christ walked out of the tomb. I ran up to him and he spoke to me."

Peters eyes got big. "What did he say? I want to hear it again. He appeared to us several times but you were the first. I have to know. What did he say?"

Tears started to run down Josiah's cheeks. "He only said a few words. 'You are forgiven.' Then he turned and walked away. We just watched him walk away."

"We?" was the quick question Peter followed with. "Patrous and myself," Josiah answered. "That is the reason he is here. The Jews tried to bribe him. I simply said to him, 'You know what you saw.'"

Patrous broke in, "I looked at Josiah and nodded at him. Then I said it's time to get to work. I resigned my commission with the Romans and we started getting together with your people. When you preached on Pentecost, we were a couple of the guys with the flame over our heads."

Peter just had one other thing to say. "You gentlemen know where this could get you, don't you? The Pharisees hate us. They thought once they had nailed Christ to the cross they had done away with him. They knew he walked out of the grave, but they don't want to give up control over the people. So they bribed the guards so they would be willing to lie about what they saw."

Patrous spoke up when he heard that. "Josiah reminded me of what I saw. I was there with him when the Christ walked out of the grave. That, my friend, is the reason I am working with him now getting the word out about what God the Father has done through the Christ."

Peter looked at the two men. He turned to his right, looked up to heaven as to say a quick prayer. He turned and walked the few paces back to his left. He then turned and looked at the two men and said, "Paul has instructed you both on why Jesus the Christ had to suffer and die so we could all walk into God the Fathers presence. You now understand fully what is at stake here. You both know where you're going to end up. It's just a matter of time until the Pharisees figure you out." With that he laid hands on the men and sent them out on the next mission the Heavenly Father had for them.

They would spend the next three days in prayer and fasting waiting to find out what the Father had for them to accomplish. They knew and understood that the commission of Jesus the Christ had given to all believers. That commission was to go out to the world. They also understood that the world could be local for some. What they did understand was that they had to be reaching out with the testimony that The Father had given them when they saw Jesus the Christ walk out of the tomb. When they heard his words, "You are forgiven," they knew and understood that these words were not just for them, but for all mankind. The other thing they knew and understood was that they could not put it off, they had to start walking and start talking. So they agreed together the next morning they would head out. Their destination unknown, but they would listen to the spirit within them and seek to see their Father in Heaven leading so as to see the lost saved. Patrous looked at Josiah. "My friend, we best go to our bedchambers. Tomorrow starts a new adventure." With that, they would both spend their last night in their own beds for a while.

The next morning, Josiah awoke to the sound of Patrous at his door. He opened the door and Patrous said, "Time to go, say goodbye to your house, we may not be coming back." Josiah smiled as he went inside to grab the few things he would take on his trip to share what he witnessed. "Peter was at my house waking me up. He told me the Holy Spirit had been nudging him to get up and get out. We have to get the message of God's forgiveness out to God's people."

As the two traveled they became more and more amazed by what the Father was doing through them. They were seeing people healed and saved daily. As they shared the forgiveness of God the Father with His people, one could see the weight of the world being lifted off of those people. When they would come out of the water after their baptism, the joy was amazing. The excitement that they felt in their heart could not be measured in human terms.

Even with all the great things that God the Father was doing through them, Josiah still had that longing to hear the words," I forgive you," from his dear sweet Anna. He knew, however, that he had to keep working because he also understood that it was not his will but the will of the Father that was important. He knew that he had to walk out the path that had been set before him. *But,* he asked himself, *what about that promise that she would evenually forgive me?*

Was that just me, or was it a promise from God?

Just then a person came across his path. He was a younger man who rushed along as if the world would run him over if he slowed down. He reached out and touched the man's shoulder. "Whoa, champ, what's the hurry?" Josiah asked.

The young man looked at him, then turned to storm off in almost a panic. Then he stopped. "Mister, you have no idea what my life is filled with. I give and give to keep people happy. The more I give the more they want. When do I get something for me?" the young man asked.

Josiah looked him straight in the eye and simply asked one question. "What are you really looking for?"

The young man was somewhat taken aback. "What do you mean what am I looking for? I am looking for something that is not attainable. I am looking for acceptance without conditions."

Josiah tilted his head slightly. Then he walked over to the man and got real close and simply said, "There is only one way to do that. You must treat others like you want to be treated."

The man responded, "Treat others like I want to be treated? Where did that come from?"

Josiah smiled. "The man who is called Jesus the Christ said it."

The man looked at Josiah and asked, "And who is this Jesus the Christ?"

"He is the Son of the Most High, He is the Son of the Great I Am," Josiah answered.

The man had an even more puzzled look on his face. "I have no idea who you are talking about."

Josiah looked over at his close friend Patrous. The look on his face said, "Help." He looked at the man he had been talking to and simply smiled as he said, "Would you excuse me for just a minute?" He turned and walked away. The man who he was talking to could see him raising his hands to heaven as he was walking and talking. But the man had to wonder who was he talking to.

Josiah was walking and praying. "Father, how do I explain to this man who you really are? He does not have a clue about you. He is ignorant of you and who you are?" He turned and walked back not knowing for sure just what the Father would have him say. He asked the man two simple questions. "My friend, have you ever done anything wrong?"

The answer came from the man quickly. "Yes."

Josiah continued, "How did you know what you did was wrong?"

The man suddenly had a strange look on his face. "I just did."

"So tell me, if you knew you did something wrong how, did you deal with it?" Josiah stated gently. "Sir, all men have sinned, none of us can stack up to the Holiness God expects of us."

The man smiled and asked one question. "How then do we get to see God?" The ulterior motive was clear on his face.

Josiah had to tell the truth. He proceeded to tell him about the Christ and how he had been the one who built the cross that Jesus the Christ was nailed to.

"So you're a believer in this Christ then?"the man asked.

"Absolutely"was the immediate answer Josiah gave.

"You believed everything they said about this rabble rouser?"the man asked.

Patrous piped in, "I nailed him to the cross, and I saw him walk out of his tomb. What more proof do you need?"

"I heard Jesus say to Nicodemus that a person must be born again. Nicodemus was not yet a believer. Yet, to everyone who truly believes and repents of their sin, he touches with His Holy Spirit and saves them. There are changed in a second forever. He is the only way to God our Father. Just before he was betrayed he prayed that God the Father would be in us as The Father is in him. He changed me forever and I made the cross they nailed him to," Josiah said.

"As I looked up to him as he died on the cross I heard him say, 'Father, forgive them for they don't know what they are doing.' I followed them as they took him to the tomb. I saw him walk out of that tomb on the third day. Then he walked up to me and said three words, 'You are forgiven.' Those words changed me in a second. My friend he is not a rabble rouser; he is the Son of the Most High God. He died and rose again. He is who he said he was. If you repent, he will save you and you can walk in his newness of life as well. It's time to stop running from God and receive the forgiveness that His Son Jesus the Christ gives through his Holy Spirit. Let us pray with you."

The man smiled. "We have got you by your words," he said with an evil laugh. "You may think I have come here to receive your 'Christ' but in reality I have come here to bring word back to the rulers of the temple and the Romans just who you are. You, Patrous, will lose your head over this, and you, Josiah, will meet the same fate as your Christ did." The man said as he turned and started to walk

away, still laughing to himself with the confidence that he helped end this new following of the Christ forever. Suddenly, he stopped dead in his tracks. The look on his face was one of question and not understanding why he stopped.

Patrous and Josiah looked at each other and shook their heads. Josiah stated, "This man has no idea that he was speaking against the Living God the Father and His

Son and His Holy Spirit. The Christ himself said that the only unforgivable sin is blasphemy against the Holy Spirit. He is walking on dangerous ground indeed."

"Yeah, but that does not help us much. We could end up losing these bodies," Patrous responded. "I don't mind dying for the Christ, but the pain that is going to be involved, I would just as soon not rush."

Josiah looked at the man who was still smiling with his evil smile. Josiah walked over to him and put his hand on his shoulder and said. "Satan, be gone from this man now in the name of Jesus the Christ!"

With that the man froze. The man then looked to the right and to the left and dropped to his knees and started to cry.

"Why did I open myself to such evil? I feel clean for the first time in years. What do I do from now on, I can't go back to the temple. They will stone me for becoming a believer in the Christ. What can I do?"

Josiah responded, "I was walking along and came across the Master teaching. He had just cast a demon out of a man. He made it clear that when a demon is cast out it will go and try to find a new dwelling place. If it can't find one it will go back to its old one with seven other demons worse than itself. I recommend you start getting yourself grounded in Christ and filled with his Holy Spirit so you will be kept clean from the enemy."

The man agreed. "Where do I start?"

Both Patrous and Josiah were very new believers. They both were, in a sense, walking in new territory.

Josiah spoke directly to the man. "We are going to meet up with Matthew and John in a couple of days. You're welcome to travel with us if you like. We will be sitting under their teaching for a week or so before we move on to spread the word."

The man looked over at Josiah and smiled as he said, "I would really appreciate that. This is a huge change for me. I want to know I made the right choice. Being taught by one who was taught from the master is above all else going to be a huge honor."

Josiah said, "The master, was not joking when he taught that we must all be willing to take up our Cross. Every day the Pharisees and Sadducees are out there to trip us up so they can send us to a cross as well."

"The fact of the matter is we have to be willing to call them out as the hypocrites that they are," Patrous added.

"I know what Christ has done in me. I feel clean and refreshed for the first time in years. The blood of the Christ even cleansed me, and I was involved in the trumping up the charges against him," the man said.

"Look, it's getting late, tomorrow is going to be a rough day as we have to push to meet as many people as God the Father through His Son by His Spirit brings across our path. We better get some sleep," Josiah said.

Josiah went into his tent and slept quickly. He fell into a deep sound sleep. As he slept, the dream that came to him was one with Anna and their children. He could feel the warmth of their son as he held the newborn in his arms and looked into the deep brown eyes of his Anna. He heard the Romans pounding at his door. He pushed Anna and their son out the back as the Roman storm troopers crashed through the front. He sat straight up in bed realizing it was a dream. He looked around in the darkness. He felt an ache in his heart as he knew that it was his love for Anna, the one who he longed for with all his heart, that could never be his. He knew the danger he would put her in and the children they would bring into the world, would be too much for him to bear.

The dream was enough for Josiah to realize that he had one choice. And that choice was to follow the Christ. He knew that he had to follow the Christ where ever that led him. He just knew that people's eternities depended on what he would do in the time that he had left on this earth. With that he rolled over and went back to sleep.

*   *   *

Meanwhile in Patrous's tent, the snoring got louder and louder. If anyone was in the tent with him the crickets outside could not be heard. The snoring got so loud the horses and donkeys started to get uneasy. Soon it became so loud that the other people in the camp woke up and not in a good mood. Josiah snuck up to his tent and signaled three other men from the camp to join him. The three of them threw open the tent, grabbed Patrous by the feet, dragged him out of the tent, and poured cold water on him and left him sputtering in the sand. Patrous slowly got up, looked around, and started to get really angry. Just then a dove landed at his feet. Patrous then looked to heaven, smiled a bit, and started to laugh. His laugh started as a chuckle, then turned to a low level laugh, then louder and louder. He was laughing so hard that the other men started to laugh as well. They all went back to their respective tents, curled up, and the night turned silent.

*   *   *

The next morning Josiah walked out of his tent. He turned to his right and there stood a man who he had never seen before. The man walked up to Josiah put his hand on his shoulder and said, "Hello, my name is Matthew. The last thing Jesus told us before he ascended to heaven was to make disciples of all nations. Baptizing them in the name of the Father and the Son and the Holy Spirit. We have to teach them all what he taught us."

Josiah got a curious look on his face. "How do we learn all that he taught? How do we make other men disciples?"

Matthew chuckled a bit, then got a very serious look on his face and said. "We walked, slept, ate, and listened to him for three and a half years. We have some scribes that are, even as we speak, writing down all that he said. We are willing to teach you so you can go out yourself and make disciples. I understand that you were there when he walked out of the tomb. You have a story to tell. But after you tell it and people come to the Christ, what then?"

Josiah shrugged. "I guess I really don't know, I heard bits and pieces of his teaching as I ran into him from time to time, but nothing in depth, looks to me you have a lot to teach me."

Matthew looked at Josiah and smiled. "We are all called to different ways of serving. Peter and Paul's main task was to lead more and more people to the Christ. Paul was being used to teach and preach and write letters to the churches around the world to build the body of Christ. What people need to understand is this. God the Father reached down into this world that had become corrupted by men's choices to sin and walk away from the Fathers best. The only problem was this: When Adam and Eve chose to walk away from what God intended there was no way back. They could cover their sin with sacrifices, but it would only cover not cleanse."

Matthew continues, "Jesus in one of his teachings said, 'I have not come to abolish the law, but fulfill it.' Jesus, Yahweh's son, was the only man ever to live a sinless life. He had to be the perfect sacrifice to pay the price for the sin that entangles man. Let me ask a question. Have you ever gone swimming and ended up having weeds tangled around your leg that just won't seem to let go?"

"I have,"Josiah answered,

"That, my friend, is what sin does. When man opens himself to it, the hold becomes a death hold. The only way to really get away from it is to have it cut out by the roots. The law required sacrifices to cover man's sin. But that would not cleanse man, only cover his sin. His sin was still there. The ultimate sacrifice was for our Father in heaven to send his Son born of a virgin to be the ultimate sacrifice."Josiah interrupted."That's why those three words that the Christ spoke to me and Patrous were able to be spoken."

Matthew asked,"What three words?"

Josiah smiled and said, "You are forgiven."

"When did he say those words to you?"Matthew asked.

"When he walked out of the tomb."

Matthew fell to his knees and started to sob. He looked to heaven, and prayed, "Father, The Lord of Heaven and Earth, I thank you that you led me here to these men. I could not understand why you had me rise in the middle of the night to be here when they woke. Now my understanding is made complete."

Matthew looked at the two men standing in front of him and said one thing, "Your commitment to the Christ has to be without waver. You can let nothing stop you on the mission the Father has put before you. You must be willing to give everything up to see other people come to the Christ and have their sins removed so they can walk into our Father's presence. You have been chosen from the beginning of time to do what he has placed you on this earth to accomplish. But you have to make a choice before you start. That choice is this. If you do this you will be killed, knowing that will you still do it?"

Patrous and Josiah looked at each other. Patrous said, "We have to die sometime. I can think of no other thing worth dying for more important than the cleansing of men's souls. That cleansing allows them to walk into the presence of God Almighty our Father, because of what His Son the Christ did by letting me nail him to the Cross that Josiah built so that we could walk in the newness of life because he walked out of the grave and told us we are forgiven."

Matthew looked at both men and said, "What you must do for a brief period of time is sit with me and learn the prophecies of old. All the words that God the Father gave to his prophet's point to one person, the Christ."

Both Josiah and Patrous looked at each other and nodded as they said in unison, "Why is it so important that we know this information?"

"It's really quite simple. The Priests and Pharisees are going to come against you with a vengeance. You must know the word of God to be able to defend yourselves. They respect the Law and the prophets only. Both the Law and the prophets point to Jesus the Christ as the Messiah. The reason they are eventually going to have the Romans kill you will be to silence you. I saw the Christ after he walked out of the tomb. You actually saw him walk out of it. If we put that together with you having knowledge of what the prophets of God Almighty said, they will not be able to argue against you. That will give you absolute credibility with the people Father brings you in contact with. Did I answer your question?"

Josiah and Patrous stated in unison, "When do we start?"

"Now is not too early," Matthew answered. "Remember this, we are at war, our weapons are not swords and spears, our weapon is the word of God himself. Our weapon is the Holy Spirit's leading that we are given daily. Our weapon does not seek to destroy lives but rebuild them. Remember this: Jesus said, 'The thief comes to kill steal and destroy, but I have come that they may have life and have it abundantly.' The enemy brings death. We bring life in Christ. Let's go."

With that, the three men began a journey that would lead them through all of the prophecies and a study of the law that would ensure two things. One, they would have an answer to every lie the leaders of the Jewish community would try to deceive the people with, and two, give them extreme credibility by sharing their eyewitness experience seeing the Christ walk out of the tomb and being able to defend why what they saw was truly the fulfillment of prophecies thousands of years old. This adds credibility for the people to grasp when they witnessed the attacks that were coming from the Jewish hierarchy.

Matthew would take the next six months cramming into their minds the prophecies of Isaiah, Jeremiah, and Joel as well as many others. He would show them from Genesis through Malachi how each book pointed to the Christ. Finally, they were ready to start an adventure that would lead to them becoming truly one with Christ, with all that it meant.

10
......
Ready for Battle

I t had been six months of intensive training. Both men had been schooled by Matthew on the prophecies of old. Both men now fully understood what they had witnessed at the cross and the tomb. But they were not prepared for the total onslaught of hell that was about to be leveled against them. But this they did know, what they had witnessed with the Christ's death and resurrection was real. It was for the redemption of mankind, and they were privileged to see it. On top of all that, because of the six months of intensive training they had done with Matthew, they now understood why God the Father did what he did. He had promised through a multitude of prophets the redeeming of mankind. They were ready to take part in the process of getting the word out to the world. Both men had resigned themselves to the fate that would eventually befall them. So in the morning they would start the final journey to see the kingdom of Christ start to take root in men's hearts.

At the same time in the temple, leaders were plotting against the believers in Christ. They had two targets. One was named Josiah and the other was Patrous. They knew these men had witnessed the death of the one called The Christ. They also knew that they had both been at the tomb when he walked out. They knew and understood that both these men had to be taken out. They knew these men had to be removed from the earth. They just had to try and figure out a way to do it that would keep their hands from having blood on them. They knew and understood that they had to "trump"up such an evil thing against them that their demise would be the natural consequence of their so-called actions. They had tried and tried to "trip"up the Christ, but never could. They figured these simple men would be very easy to trip up.

What they did not realize was that Matthew, the disciple of Christ, had been training these men in the prophecies of old as well as the new teachings of the Christ. Christ had stated himself that he had not come to abolish the law, but that the law would be fulfilled through him. One extremely valuable thing that they had been taught was to answer a question with a question. This technique had been taught by example by the Christ himself.

As the two men walked and talked to more and more people they were seeing the power of the Spirit of God himself start to work in people's lives. The leaders of the temple saw the same thing, and that was going to be a problem for Josiah and Patrous. As the two were standing in the street surrounded by people listening to their eyewitness account of what happened when they were confronted by Jewish priests.

"Who gives you the authority to speak in the name of this 'Jesus' you talk about?" they screamed! hoping to trip them up. Josiah looked at them and simply said, "You answer my question first. When the veil of the temple was torn at the very second of the death of Jesus the Christ, where did the Spirit of God go? You hypocrites, you search the scriptures for the prophecies and see if Jesus did not fulfill them all. Yet you won't accept his lordship because you would have to give up your power over the people. You bask in your power, yet the people suffer and are pulled more away from God the Father because you want to maintain that power. Jesus the only begotten Son of God came to set men free. You're one of the things he came to set men and women free from. His promise that man would be the dwelling place of the spirit takes them away from your power over them. Read the prophets. You will see over and over again that they point to the Christ as the messiah. God the Father is not interested in earthly kingdoms. God the Father is interested in His kingdom. My suggestion to you is to read what he had his prophets say. My suggestion to you is to take a look at the truths that are written by the prophets. My suggestion is to put those truths to work in your lives. My suggestion is to stop attacking the very people that God sent his Christ to save and accept the Christ into your own hearts and lives."

The men in their fancy robes became hot with anger. They had just been shut down. The Holy Spirit himself had given Josiah the words needed to shut these men out for the moment. The very words of hope that Josiah spoke were the words that they saw as taking their power away. They turned to each other with one purpose in mind. They had to take these two men out before more of their precious flock of people who they had under their thumbs followed the Christ. They knew and understood that their power rested in the people who realized they had the only path to God. They knew the Christ had given men the true path to knowing God in a real way. They understood what really happened when the curtain blocking the Holy of Holies was torn from top to bottom. The also understood that the power they were addicted to would be taken from them if they did not cover up what they knew.

That left them only one thing to do. They had to figure out a way to "get rid" of them just like they did with the Christ. This would not be an easy task as more and more of the Jews were starting to follow the teachings these men. They were seeing lives changed and did not know how to stop it. They realized their power did not come from the love of God, but a dread fear of him.

The new teachings from Josiah and Patrous was teaching that God so loved the world that he gave his only Son, that whoever believed on him would not perish but have everlasting life. This teaching was taking their petri-fied flock and making them brave as lions. They knew in their hearts that to do nothing would leave them without any hope of loosening the control the Jewish leaders over the people.

They understood where their power came   from. They knew the prophecies and they understood that Christ fulfilled them.

The Jewish leaders also understood that the power they had was no longer from God, but they could and would not give it up without a fight. They knew their power against the power of the Christ who had walked out of the grave was something that they would surely lose. What they did not understand was the power of forgiveness that the Christ taught his followers.

*   *   *

Nicodemus had been there with them when the one they called Jesus the Christ had taught his disciples to pray. He could not understand why anyone would teach his followers to pray. "Forgive us as we have forgiven those who have trespassed against us." He turned and walked over to his servant. He gave the servant orders that both Josiah and Patrous be brought to him.

Two days later, Josiah and Patrous were brought into Nicodemus's quarters.

"Gentlemen, I need to know what you're telling the people," Nicodemus stated in a demanding tone of voice.

Josiah answered with a tone of defiant authority. "We are teaching what the Christ taught. We are teaching for-giveness by the blood of Christ. We are teaching that man can have his sins washed away and be set free from all that tangles him up."

Nicodemus understood the Christ. He knew he was who he said he was just from the time when he heard the

Christ tell him directly that he must be born again. He knew that somehow he had to have his spirit made new. He just never did figure out how to do it.

"Josiah," Nicodemus said, "you have spent considerable time with his follower Peter. Can you please tell me now how to I gain the spiritual rebirth?"

"What did the Christ tell you at your home?" Josiah asked.

"He said a lot of things. Whoever believes on him will not perish but have life everlasting. He said he who does not believe is condemned already. The Christ stated that he who loves darkness is condemned. He also stated many other things. One of the other things was that you must be born again. How do I do that?"

Patrous chimed in, "Jesus did say the he who confesses me before men I will confess before my Father in heaven. First you must confess your sins and pray that Jesus be your lord and savior. Then, Nicodemus, my friend, it's time you go and start talking to the Pharisees and show them the prophecies and start showing them that Christ really is who he said he is."

"How can I do that? If I make that kind of confession they will throw me out of the temple," Nicodemus said.

"The Christ said that many men love the approval of men more than the approval of God. Nicodemus, are you one of those people? We all have choices to make. But, Nicodemus, your eternity depends on your answer. You read the prophecies. You know what the word of God said, and you know what the Christ told you when you spoke with him. Josiah and I saw him walk out of the grave. He spoke to us. He told us we were forgiven. We cannot help but tell the world what Christ had done for us. The question is this: What are you going to do with all of this?"

Nicodemus got a worried look on his face. "If I confess him they will probably kick me out of the temple or worse, kick me out and have me nailed to one of those crosses. Gentleman, I am scared of what will happen."

Josiah answered, "So what I hear you telling me is that you fear man more than God. Remember what Jesus said. 'Don't fear them who can kill your body. I tell you fear him who after he kills the body has the power to cast your soul into hell.'"

Nicodemus started walking around in circles and looked to heaven. "Father, what am I supposed to do? Where do you want me? Do you want me to go and confess you before the council?"

Just then he could hear the words of the Christ as if he was standing beside him. "He who confesses me before men I will confess before my Father who is in heaven."

It was from this point forward that Nicodemus would not ever compromise what he knew to be true. He would be baptized as the public show of his faith, and he would use his wealth to help further the gospel of the Christ.

Nicodemus looked at Josiah and Patrous. "I think, gen-tlemen, it's time we go to war. As I see it we have some weapons that we must be aware of. One, we have the prophecies. Two, we have the Spirit of God within us. Three, you two witnessed his resurrection. There is nothing more convincing than eyewitness testimony. But remember the leaders of the Jews can be quite vicious.

Remember, we fight not against flesh and blood but, against rulers and principalities that are of Satan himself. This war is not to gain ground on this earth. This war is to save men's and women's souls for eternity. This war will not be lost. The ultimate victory is God the Father's though his Son the Christ by His Holy Spirit. The leaders of the temple don't know God. They have turned their back on him, and became controlled by their own greed for power. God the Father is about to break that. Christ spoke to them directly when he told them they have a form of Godliness but denied the power thereof. Gentlemen it's time to go to work."

With that the three men set their eyes on the kingdom and got ready for the ultimate battle for the hearts and minds of every living person on the earth. They knew what their physical end on this earth would be. They were ready for it. They knelt and prayed for the blessings of the Most High and got ready for the next morning when the war would begin in earnest for the lives of God's people.

11
. . . . . .
The War Heats Up

Josiah and Patrous were standing in the road talking to fellow Jews about the Messiah Jesus. The man and woman they were talking to were listening intently. Suddenly both men at the same moment felt arms around them and ropes tying their hands and feet. They realized they were being hauled off to prison for preaching about the Christ in public.

Josiah heard a warm loving voice say, "Don't panic." He looked up toward the sky and simply smiled.

They knew that the war for men's and women's hearts was underway. They also knew what the chief weapon would be. That weapon would be two simple words. Those weapons would be prayer and worship.

*   *   *

They soon found themselves thrown into a prison with a couple of other Christians.

They looked at each other shackled to the floor. Josiah and Patrous and Peter and Barnabas. The guards were sleeping in the same cell with them. They could feel the prayers of the fellow believers going up to the throne room of God the Father.

Suddenly through the closed cell door the angel came. Their chains fell off. They found themselves free, all they had to do was get up and walk out. They looked at each other, they were about to not get up as they knew what would happen to the guards. It would mean their death. They hesitated. But the Angel of God Most High made it clear that God was not done with them and they had to leave. NOW!

As they walked away the Josiah asked Peter. "What caused the chains to fall?"

Peter looked at Josiah and Patrous and smiled. "That, my brother, was the prayers of the believers. God in heaven heard them and answered. We are now free. At least for a while. Our Father in heaven has work for us to do yet. We have to spread the word of what Christ has done for us by his sacrifice on the Cross. We are at war for men's souls. Our weapons are not swords, our weapons are the Word of God, prayer, and worship. Our weapons don't win by destroying lives, our weapons win by rebuilding them."

As they made their way back to Mary's house they began discussing the parable that the Christ told them about a Pharisee and a tax collector.

*   *   *

Josiah said, "All these years we have been taught that honor went with the robes. Christ taught us that true honor comes from God our Father because of a broken and contrite heart. He taught us that to really live we must be a servant. We must be able to put others before ourselves. That is not always an easy thing to do. But we must do it."

At that second Josiah looked up and saw Anna. She smiled at him. He wanted with all his heart to have conversation with her but felt stopped. He could not understand if it was God's Spirit stopping him, or his own fear. He wanted to express his deepest desire to be close to her. But something stopped him. She turned and walked away, and his heart sank. It was time to get back to work. It was time to continue on the journey to Mary's home. But he could not get rid of the longing to be close to Anna. He had a deep desire for more. He knew his commitment to the Kingdom meant letting go of some things. He understood that the desire for that one companion was out of the question. His commitment to seeing more and more people come to that understanding and experiencing the Risen Christ was and had to be his driving force in all that he did. Yet the longing was there to hear a sweat voice beside him in the morning. The longing to be held by the love of his life at night would not go away. He had a deep longing to be able to love and be loved by one person who he knew he would never have, Anna.

*   *   *

Josiah shook his head to bring himself back to reality. God the Father had placed him in the company of Peter for a   reason. That reason was to come to an understanding of what his weapons of warfare were and not to allow himself to be drawn into self-pity. His understanding was starting to become awakened to what the weapon of his warfare would be.

He realized that the Christ had been willing to suffer the pain and humiliation of the Cross for Him. He began to realize as he was taught more and more of the Christ, and that his giving to the people that knowledge of what the Christ had done, would be what would change those people forever. The words that Jesus had said, "As you have done it to the least of these you have done it to me," began to ring in his ears.

His mind would go back to when he was working in the fields. He was scratching out a living wondering what it would be like to be rich. Josiah simply stopped. He began to understand what real riches were. They were not to be found in silver and gold, but in the giving heart of the Christ.

His thoughts then went to the last prayer of the Christ in the Garden before going to the Cross he built that would take his physical life. Peter had told him of the prayer and how the Christ had prayed that the Father would be in the believers as the Father was in him. Suddenly a light went on inside his mind. If God's Holy Spirit was in him, that meant that his newfound need to give was from

God Almighty himself, which led to another conclusion. That God the Father had given his only begotten Son not to condemn the world, but to save it. His mind went back to that Sunday morning at the tomb when he and Patrous had witnessed the Christ walk out of the tomb. He remembered those piercing eyes looking into his as he said those three words that would change his life and the lives of millions of people who would hear them in the years to come. "You are forgiven." Those three words are what cleansed man's heart and mind so the spirit could dwell in him. What God gave would become extremely important in the mind of Josiah and in the hearts of all those who accepted Christ's salvation.

The next morning Josiah walked over to Patrous's tent. "My brother, it's time to get up and prepare for the glorious day that the Lord has made," he said in an extremely cheerful tone. "I have been shown what our weapons of war are, we will be given victories, the enemy of men's souls has been defeated."

He started to sing. "God has spoken to his people and his words are words of wisdom." He sang the tune louder and louder until Patrous climbed out of his tent.

Josiah took one look at Patrous and started to chuckle, that chuckle would get a bit louder and louder until it became gutwrenching laughter. He looked at Patrous and the normally clean-cut military appearance coming out of his tent with a cap that looked like a strange bird sitting on his head. The big red eyes protruding out of the sockets of the bird drew an emotion out of Josiah that he had not felt in a long time. The laughter in his gut felt like such a release that he was amazed at the cleansing he felt. He looked to heaven and felt the laughing eyes of the Father looking down on him. He knew that what was written about laughter being good medicine was true.

Patrous had laughed so hard he had tears running down his cheeks. He looked at Josiah and gave him a smile. "Now, my friend, it's time for us to get ready to attack the enemy of people's souls. It's time to see people's hearts changed by the power of the Most High and witness lives become one with the Father through His Son the Christ.

"The thing to keep in mind is this. Our Father in heaven is sovereign, he is going to save people through the blood of His son the Christ. He is going to make his presence known, remember this, none of the people in this place were there on Pentecost and none have asked to be filled with the Holy Spirit. Also, remember this, Jesus when he prayed in the Garden asked that as the Father was in him that he would be in us. On Pentecost that prayer was answered. That is the strongest weapon of our warfare. We have God the Father's Holy Spirit dwelling within us. Because of that, we have instant communication with the Father. My brother, it's time to go to war!" Petrous said.

As Josiah turned to walk away, he ran into Anna who had been looking for him for some time.

Anna with her big brown eyes looked into Josiah eyes and said. "Canwetalk?"

Josiah, without a word, reached out took her hand, and said, "Let's walk."

The two held hands and walked for hours. Silence enveloped them. Josiah stopped and turned Anna toward himself. Looked into big brown eyes and simply smiled. "I think we had better head back now."

Anna looked at him and smiled. "Tell me why?" she said .

Josiah knew what he had to do. The dream he had for himself and what he wanted, he knew could never be. "Anna, what I did by building those crosses is almost unforgivable. I won't ask you, I just think that it is better for both of us if we don't go anywhere with this. Father has things for me to accomplish that are going to bring many of His people into His kingdom. It may not be pretty where I end up. You have to be safe as I know Father has a role for you in his purpose as well. But, Anna, I have to ask you one question. I am trying to understand all of the weapons that we have. You listened to the Christ a great deal when he was on this earth, did you not?"

Anna in her sweet voice gave a simple yes.

Josiah continued his question. "Tell me, did you hear him speak a parable on talents?"

Anna smiled as she answered, "Yes, I did. It went something like this. A rich man was going away on a trip. He gave to one five, another three, and a third one. In this parable he spoke to those of us listening about the landowner is the Father. We are the servants, and the talents are our gifts. The first two men doubled their talents before the landowner got back. However, the third man hid his talent. He was afraid of the master so he hid it so he would not lose it. The landowner condemned him."

"Anna, let's walk some more. I need to talk this out. If I am hearing you right, and I think I am, we are all given gifts, right?"

"That is correct. Some more than others. It's what we do with them that counts. We have to use our gifts to advance the kingdom by spreading the word of God to anyone who will hear it. We can do that by using our gifts. For instance, if we have the ability to build things, as you do, we can help someone who really needs it. When we do this that person may become open to what we are saying because we are putting our Faith into action. So, my friend, what you could have done, instead of building things that killed freedom fighters, you could have built a porch or a chair. You would then see people open their hearts to what you have to say about the kingdom," Anna said with a tone of resentment in her voice.

Josiah's face became red with shame as he said, "Anna, Christ forgave me. Can't you? Somehow we have to get by this."

Anna started to cry as she screamed at Josiah, "My brother was nailed to one of those damnable trees. You may have made it. And you want me to forgive you? I am not the Christ." She fumed as she stormed off.

Josiah became instantly enraged. He looked up to heaven shaking his fist. Not this time at God the Father, but this time with a determination to totally defeat the enemy through the power of the Christ Crucified. He had seen the power of the Christ. He remembered how he allowed himself to be used by the enemy of his soul to destroy God's people. His focus would be that of a warrior getting ready to attack an enemy that was out to destroy his people. He knew one thing. They had to get ready to mount an attack and watch the destruction of the enemy's world begin.

12

The Great Battle Begins

Patrous was standing beside Josiah. "Man, you're looking off into space like something is really bothering you," he said.

Josiah shrugged as he answered, "Just some personal stuff. I am getting hit over and over again with just how evil making those crosses really was. Christ paid the price needed to stop the enemy of man's soul. The beauty of the whole thing is all man had to do was say yes to the Christ and be baptized and he would be saved. We are just two of the vehicles that our Father in Heaven will use to stop him. I think our Father is leading us away from the temple. I think we are to be headed for Rome. We have to remember this. We have messed up big time. I feel like I had a hand in murdering a lot of good men. Feel like! I did have a part in the murder of a lot of good men. But the Christ forgave me for all of it. If he could forgive me for committing the worst crime possible against his people, he can forgive those he brings us in contact with. That's the story we tell. That's our weapon of warfare. We have to remember this. St. Paul said that our Father in heaven works all things for the Good to those who love God and are called according to His purpose."

Patrous looked at Josiah and said, "My friend, we have our work cut out for us. We have worked with Peter. We have been taught by Paul as he taught us the prophecies that all pointed to the Christ. Now it's time for us to go to work and share the knowledge we have been given and our testimonies with those we come in contact with. The question I have is this. How do we do that? How do we take all that we have been given and put it into practical use?"

Josiah said one thing. "Let's pray."

With that the two men spent the next two hours in prayer. On their knees, walking around, and sitting. They spent the time seeking the Face of the Father through the Son by his Holy Spirit. They sought to know where their mission field was. The more they prayed and sought the more they were led to the same conclusion. They had to start a business. Not just any business, but one that would bring Glory to the Father through the Son. One that would help people, and one that would bring people closer to what Father wanted in their lives.

Patrous looked at Josiah and asked, "What, my friend, do you think we should do? What kind of business can we get into? I have built a career on being a soldier. You have built crosses. What can we do with those kinds of experiences?"

Josiah looked at Patrous and simply said, "You know how to take command of a situation, do you not? I would suggest that you are going to be the one who runs the shop. What I really sense is that our Father wants us to fill the shop with crosses. Those crosses will be worn by people who just can't seem to get it together. Those people who are just passed by. And our Father will turn them into people of beauty. Our Father will create something that will draw more people to the one who created them in the first place. When Jesus walked on this earth created miracles. He will show us those who God created with the gifts of being able to work with their hands and hearts. He will take those gifts and create pieces that are so beautiful that people will be drawn to them. When people buy them they will be asking what each piece means. That's when we will be able to share what Father has changed our lives and the lives of those working for us."

Patrous asked a couple of questions. "Where are we going to set up this shop? Where are we going to find these men? And how are we going to pay for getting all of this started?"

Josiah smiled as he knew the answer to each question. "My friend. My dear friend, who I love like a brother. They paid lots of money for the hundreds of crosses that I built. The psalmist wrote: 'What the enemy meant for evil the Father means for good.' That is our startup money. Christ told us to go to the highway and byways. That's where we will find the people he has chosen for us. Lastly, I have a huge barn on my property that will work very nicely as our factory for building those things that will touch the lives of those around us." What are we going to build?" Patrous asked.

"We are going to turn the ugliness of the Cross into a thing of beauty. We are saved by the death of Christ on the Cross. We have been given life eternal through the Cross. And we are given new life through the Holy Spirit. I saw a dove land on my window sill. In my mind that represents the Holy Spirit. We will make doves and crosses that people will wear around their necks. It is the Cross that is going to help fund the activities of those who God is sending to spread the word."

Patrous got a quizzical look on his face. "What is it that you have in mind?"

"From my first memories I have seen the Ark of the Covenant. We are now moving into an age of grace. The Ark stands for man's working to achieve forgiveness from God. The Cross represents that forgiveness that has been paid for by God's sacrifice of his Son. As we start making small crosses that can be worn around the people's necks, people will start asking people why they wear them. The answers are going to get people's attention. We will make crosses that people can put in their houses and wear around their neck. And, my friend, know this. There will be a story behind every cross."

Patrous got a worried look on his face. "Josiah, you know we have been ordered not even to speak the Name of Christ. Do you understand where this is going to end up?"

Josiah knew exactly how to respond to the question. "Remember when Peter told us about what happened when the Christ went to John to be baptized? Just before Jesus the Christ showed up, John said that there was one coming after him whose shoes he was not worthy to untie."

He then continued, "The one coming after him would not baptize with water as he did, but with the Holy Spirit and with fire. My friend it may be time for our baptism with fire."

Josiah continued, "We both have been given talents. I used mine for evil. Now our Father is going to use them for His greatness." With that he directed Patrous over to the drafting table he had put together. On it he had simple wooden crosses drawn out. He then directed him over to more complex altars that could be used in their homes. He also showed him simple wooden cups he put together for celebration of Passover and the last supper. He then took him into his "Ark" room.

Patrous had to ask one question. The answer would be a bit more complex. "Why the Arks?"

Josiah smiled as he said, "God has provided Arks for protection for his people over the centuries. The two that we are dealing with protected those who lived by the Word of God. The first Noah built when he was over six hundred years old. God used it to save not only man but his whole creation. The part of mankind that he saved lived by his word. The second housed the law that was given to Moses. The cross represents the third. Christ, you see, makes us clean so the Holy Spirit can reside within us. Man's heart becomes an Ark for the word of God. Man becomes the dwelling place of the Holy Spirit. Hence the term Ark could be used for each of our hearts. The reason God tore the veil in the temple was because the Holy Spirit left. No longer would God's Ark be made by man's hands, but by the Holy Spirit when someone receives Chris as their savior. At that point man's heart becomes the 'New Ark of the New Covenant.' As we study the word of Yahweh and His word permeates our hearts our 'Ark' will become fuller and fuller."

Patrous started to look dumbfounded. "Look, Josiah, I am just a humble soldier. I don't know all of that doctrine stuff. I do know what I saw. I saw a dead man that I had nailed to a cross get up and walk out of the grave. I heard him tell me I was forgiven. What does all this Ark stuff mean to me?"

Josiah said, "I will make this as simple for you as I can, Patrous. I will break it down as easy to understand as possible. Man sinned. God cannot have anything that is not pure and Holy in his presence. Man became more and more sinful. God wiped mankind out with a flood. He used Noah to build an ark to save man from the flood. That was the first Ark. The second Ark was the Ark of the Covenant. In that Ark of the Covenant, God the Father would put his covenant that he made with his people. This, of course, was his law. It was understood if man could keep the law it would save him. The only problem that was something man could not do in his sinful state. What the Father then had to do was cleanse man. The only way to do that was to have a perfect sacrifice. This would not be one made with wood or even gold. This Ark would be one made with blood. Not the blood of an ani-mal but one made with the blood of God's only Son the Christ. Once the vessel, man's heart, was cleansed then God's Holy Spirit could take up residence there."

Josiah continued, "Remember the veil of the temple? It was ripped in two the moment the Christ's heart stopped beating. That was the second that God's spirit would never again dwell in things made by man's hands. God's Spirit from that point on would dwell in men's hearts."

Patrous answered with another question. "So what I hear you saying is this. Because of the sacrifice Jesus the Christ made for us on the cross, God's spirit now can indwell mankind, is that correct?"

"Yes, you have got it!" was the instant response from Josiah. "Instead of God dwelling in a building or an Ark stored in the building, God the Father through His Son Jesus the Christ now indwells mankind himself. But, it is up to man to allow the Holy Spirit to take up that dwelling place. That does not happen without the blood Christ shed on the Cross cleansing man."

"I know I am forgiven. I was there and the Christ told me I was forgiven. But how does someone who was not standing at the tomb when the Christ walked out and heard him speak to them know he is forgiven?" Patrous asked.

"Simple. All they have to do is ask. I was talking to John. John was in the garden with Jesus as he was praying his last prayer before he was brought to you and you nailed him to the cross I built. He heard the Christ pray that we would be one with God the Father as he is. That's a pretty close relationship. We can now do that because of the Spirit of God Himself dwelling within us."

"So we become the weapon that God the Father uses to destroy the enemy?" Patrous said.

"Not at all. The weapon he uses to destroy the enemies' plans is the blood of Christ that we helped shed on the cross. That is what cleanses people's souls of the sin that ties them from head to foot. All man has to do to be cleansed is receive the cleansing. Remember Jesus told Nicodemus all one had to do was believe and be baptized and he would be saved. Christ's blood is like clear water that has been placed in a basin to wash a child. This child has been playing all day and does not want to come in from the dirt that they have been playing in. The parent has to go and find the child to get them cleansed. The child stops running away from the parent and jumps into their loving arms. The parent then is able to cleanse the child from all the dirt the world has thrown on them. That my friend is what happens when a person stops running and receives the forgiveness that Christ offers.

"This I can tell you. When that person stops running is when the ultimate victory is the Father's. That is when the price that the Christ paid on the Cross buys the salvation of the one who receives the free gift that Christ paid for. But that battle is not the end of the War. What the Father has done is just enlisted into his service another warrior to work toward the total defeat of the enemy. My friend, that's where we are at right now. Father has us in exactly the position he wants us to mount an attack.

"Remember this. The Pharisees power was in the Ark of the Covenant. God the Father gave Moses the Law so man's sin could be covered. Those commandments are kept in that Arc. Christ' sacrifice on the cross made them worthless to them.

All of those laws were fulfilled by what the Christ did on the cross.

"The crosses that people will have in their homes, and wear around their neck will remind the Pharisees that the enemies' power is broken. The profits we make from them will be reinvested back into the kingdom."

Patrous responded, "So where does our trial by fire come in?"

13
. . . . . .
Trial by Fire

It was dawn. Josiah had woken early to start building "crosses." He went out to his old work shed and just stood in the silence. He looked at the two crosses that were leaned up against a wall and thought back to the one they took for the Christ. He closed his eyes. He could almost see the badly beaten Christ as they threw the cross down on the ground and tied him to the death tree, then nailed him to it. He could hear the screams of those on either side of him, but the Christ somehow was able to hold it. There were no screams as they drove the nails into his palms and as they had tied his arms to the tree so not to tear the hand from the middle out. He could almost see the tears running down his cheeks because he knew the price he was paying for the redemption of mankind. Then his mind snapped him back to the present. He grabbed the cross that was leaning against the wall and started to chop pieces out of it that could be fashioned into small replicas of the cross.

He would spend the next several hours just trying to get the right cut. He knew what he was being led to do. It had to be a symbol that fellow believers would recognize and know that a true believer was standing in front of him. He looked at the models he had drawn on paper. He envisioned a young woman wearing it as a necklace. He then could see a man with a more masculine form around his neck. Josiah spent the next several hours smoothing out each little cross. Late into the night he worked. With each move over the small pieces of wood he knew he was getting closer and closer to where he needed it to be. He was starting to feel more and more driven. He knew it was the Holy Spirit that was driving him to help with the silent communication process that would be a sign for the believers for thousands of years to come. Then it happened, the knock on his door. His first customer was knocking. It was Anna, dear sweet Anna. He opened the door and said, "Please come in." Anna walked in, anger still in her spirit. She looked at the little crosses that Josiah had been working on. "Why are you making these things? Was it not enough that you made the real ones that they nailed our freedom fighters too. Not to mention you built the cross that they nailed the best man ever to walk this earth, Jesus to!"

Josiah looked deeply into Anna's eyes as he said, "Look, Anna, what I did was wrong. I admit what I did was wrong. I have repented of the wrong I have done. I was there when Jesus walked out of the tomb. He spoke three words to me. He told me I was forgiven. Anna all you have to do is look into the writing of Isaiah and you will see the type of death the Christ had to die. At the second he died the veil in the temple was torn. The Holy Spirit was given to man. The Holy Spirit would no longer dwell in a stone building but in man's hearts the way that God intended it before Adam's fall. If he could forgive me, can't you?"

Anger flashed across Anna's face as she said, "Josiah, you just don't get it. You betrayed your people. You just did not sin against Jesus building those crosses they nailed our freedom fighters to, you betrayed your own people. You became wealthy by the blood of the martyrs. You sold out your own people for thirty pieces of silver per life. Have you no shame for what you have done? Give me one of those crosses. I will wear it so other believers can recognize me as a believer. But to forgive you for what you have done to my people and my brother will not happen. Jesus may have forgiven you for what you have done, but I am not Jesus. You also tried to deceive me from the get-go. You would have pulled me into your sin if you could. You tried to get me to fall in love with you, then you would have shown me where you got you wealth. How much do I owe you for it?"

Josiah answered. "It's a gift, just take it."

Anna shook her head in more intense anger. "I don't want your gifts. You killed my people and my brother. How much do I pay you?"

He told Anna that the cross she wanted was one-half denarii. She paid him and left. Josiah looked at the small coin in his hand. Tears started to run down his cheek as he just took a few steps. He realized that he had lost a woman who would have been a great helpmate for what the Father through His Son by His Spirit that indwelt him was going to be leading him into. He also realized that if she were to forgive him, really forgive him, perhaps they could start the whole thing over again and see a future together. He just did not know if that would be possible ever. But one thing he knew about his heavenly Father. If it would work to fulfill the Father's purpose, anything was possible and nothing was impossible.

Josiah continued on with his work. Hour after long hour he would spend on a single piece. He would make every little cross perfect. He would make sure that each piece would be finished in such a way as to bring glory to the Father through His Son by His Holy Spirit. People would come to the door to buy the little crosses then leave. He would not be able to build relationships with them. But he knew that by them wearing those small crosses around their neck that those around them who were believers as well could help build relationship with them.

He was just about to close up shop for the day when the doors blew open. Temple guards stormed in. They dumped the tables that Josiah had been working on and threw the crosses that he had been working on onto the floor. Tables were flying everywhere as well as his tools and supplies. All Josiah could do was stand there and watch. When they left they told him to stop with the crosses. They also told him they knew he was a witness to the Risen Christ. But he had better keep quiet.

Josiah looked at them intensely. He turned to his right and stepped over the huge mess they had created in his work shop. He turned back and looked at them as the high priest walked in. His gold studded robes flowed as he walked into the room. Josiah had just a slight smile cross his lips as he sensed exactly what the Holy Spirit wanted him to say. "You know what God the Father had Isaiah write. The messiah had to be nailed to a cross. He had to die for the sins of many. Yet you choose to neglect the very Messiah that you have been praying for all of those years. Do you realize the power that God the Father would bestow on you to use for building his kingdom if you would only accept the forgiveness that He is offering you through the Christ? You know and understand that God's Holy Spirit left the Holy of Holies when the veil was torn. Things don't happen by accident, everything is planned for the redemption of man. That's what this is all about. I know what you are really worried about. You are worried about your temporal power. If I were you I would not worry about it too much. God the Father through His Son by His Holy Spirit is going to take the power you now have and rip it from you. The Christ called you blind guides. And so you are. God the Father will not stand for you keeping his children from getting to know him in an intimate and personal way."

The redness in the face of the High Priest showed the anger he was feeling.

He cursed Josiah and left with his guards. Patrous walked in at the same time the high priest walked out. He looked around to see the damage they had done.

"What just happened here?" he asked with a look of being totally dumbfounded.

"We just got raided by the temple guard. It appears that Christ is having an effect on the power structure of the temple. When God the Father tore the veil, at that time, it seems to me, that his spirit left the temple to live in men's hearts. What is going on here is going to change the world and we are part of it," Josiah responded. "The priests see their power over the people disappearing if they don't have a part in man's redemption. For them to maintain their power they have to control us. They have to try to nip in the bud what God the Father through His Son by His Spirit is doing here. This may not end pretty for us, but God the Father cannot be stopped," Josiah continued.

"What they don't realize is where the real power is. Remember Joseph in Genesis? At the very end of the book his brothers came back. They had thrown him in the pit out of jealousy. Then they sold him into slavery by selling him to the Egyptians. When the brothers came to Joseph he forgave them. He told them what Satan meant for evil God meant for good," he said, looking at Patrous.

Patrous shook his head as he answered with a question. "Where is this going to end? They seem to have one goal in life now. That goal is to stop the growth of God the Father through His Son by his Spirit's church. They seem to hate God the Father now. But the only way they seem to be able to maintain their control is by promoting a lie. The tried to bribe me at the tomb and to say I fell asleep. I don't fall asleep on guard. I saw the Christ walk out of the grave. I looked him in the eye. I heard him say those words that changed my life. 'You are forgiven.' Then I saw him walk away, very much alive." He got up from the chair he was sitting in and walked across the room.

Josiah looked around the room as Patrous walked through all of the tables that had been turned over again. "My friend, it seems to me that we must be having a huge effect on their power. I think the people must be asking them more and more question about the prophesies that were written and fulfilled. We just have to get this put back together and get on with what the Father is leading us to do."

With that the two men put the tables back where they needed to be. They fixed the saw that had been damaged. Then Josiah was able to get back to work making more crosses and doves. Josiah and Patrous spent the next few hours working with the wood. Shaving it, rubbing it, and getting it ready to be made into the symbols of the believer's new faith in the Risen Christ. They both knew and understood that the believers had to know who their fellow believers were. They had to get word to Peter what the rulers of the temple were doing to try to snuff out the believers. They knew the threat that the Risen Christ put forth for the leaders of the temple.

*   *   *

There was a knock at the door. Josiah opened it carefully and Peter was outside. He ushered him in and proceeded to tell him all that had happened with the leaders of the temple. Peter nodded his head as he understood completely what had happened. He would explain to them the complete history of what happened from the beginning of time.

Peter said, "God the Father no longer dwells in the Holy of Holies. He now dwells in the beings he created. Christ's prayer in the Garden was that the Father would be in man as in Christ. The Holy Spirit would never again be in a building, or a wood Ark. The Holy Spirit would be now in man as he was when God the Father breathed into the first man, Adam. They knew the prophecies that were written. They were very learned men. Their knowledge was almost their shortfall. They knew that the Christ would come to set the captives free. Jesus is the one who is now setting the captives free. The problem is they are some of the biggest captors. Jesus called them hypocrites, blind guides. He threw them out of the temple. You gentlemen scare them. You're going to take away their power base. You're going to take away the ones who pay them. They don't have their eye on the kingdom of God their eyes are on their money pouches."

Josiah and Patrous just stood across from Peter shaking their heads. "What can we do to stop them?" Josiah asked.

Peter simply said, "God the Father through his Son Jesus and by His Holy Spirit is putting huge conviction on them. The Father will stop them cold. They know the truth of who Jesus is. The problem is, they lie to themselves, so they can justify in their own minds the lies their telling the common folks. When Jesus said it would be better for them to have a millstone tied around their neck and be thrown into the sea than to cause one of His little ones to stumble, he was, not just talking about young children, although that is the emphasis. He was talking about those children of his that the leaders of the Temple are leading astray."

Peter continued, "What we have to keep in mind is this, there was a reason Christ told us to go into the whole world and share the good news that God came down in the person of Jesus to set them free from all of their sin. But be prepared to be condemned for what God was asking us to do. That condemnation is not from God, it's from man. Paul wrote in one of his letters, to live is Christ and to die is gain. We win either way."

All three of the men knew and understood that the battle was going to get hot. They knew and understood that it was for men and women's lives on this earth, but even more important their eternity. They realized that Christ had died to set mankind free from the law of sin and death. They also knew that it could end up in their death on this earth. But as they looked at each other, they came to a realization that they would all see death in one way or another if the Christ did not return first. Silently they communicated with each other standing in the work shop. The crosses still had to be built. Lives had to be touched and the power of the Christ would be used to touch more and more lives.

14

······

Total Victory Is the Lord's

Josiah and Patrous were walking down a dusty street in Jerusalem. As they approached the temple they could see a commotion on the steps. They saw Peter and John being threatened by the priests. As they had been walking up to pray, they saw a lame man on the temple grounds begging. They looked at him and said one truth, "Silver and gold we don't have, but what we do have we will gladly give to you. In the name of Jesus the Christ rise up and walk!"

They then took him by the hand and he stood up. He then started to run and leap and praised the name of the Lord. People all around were amazed at the greatness of God the Father through Jesus the Christ that was being demonstrated by these two men. The people started to sing in the streets. People were being drawn to the Christ, because of what God the Father had done through Peter and John. Josiah and Patrous could only smile as they understood what was happening. God the Father through His son the Christ by His Holy Spirit was leading His men to do things that would shake the people's confidence in the Jewish leadership. God the Father was not moving in the temple, since he had left the Holy of Holies, the High Priest was simply going through the motions of the sacrifice. They still used it as a means of control for the people, yet all their sacrifices were useless because the total sacrifice had been done when they nailed the Christ to the cross and he walked out of the grave.

Josiah and Patrous knew and understood what it meant. Men were not set free by killing animals and burning them on the altar. Men were being set free by the redemptive powers of the Christ. Person after person was becoming totally cleansed by the power of the Holy Spirit that would fill them. Since Pentecost they had all come to realize that the real power was the Christ living inside them. They would see people's lives changed in a second. Drunks would quit drinking. Sinners would quit sinning. Thieves would quit stealing. The old order had passed away. People were being changed. The Priest power was being taken from them. One symbol of this was the crosses and doves that Josiah was making and people were wearing around their neck.

When priests and the rulers of the temple would walk down the street and see people wearing the symbols that Josiah had made, the anger in their hearts would burn red. They could think of only one thing. That thing was the death of both Josiah and Patrous. They knew that trumping up charges against them would be easier than it was with the Jesus the Christ, but they also understood that it had to be done in such a way that it could not be attributed to them.

They went behind closed doors to hatch the plot.

In the meantime, Peter and John were busy ministering to God's people. The Hebrew people were accepting Jesus as their Messiah in droves. But, the more people came to Christ, the more, the hatred for the disciples grew, causing the hatred for the people who accepted Christ from hearing their testimony to be hated as well.

It seemed that the power lost by the Chief Priest and Pharisees was getting them to a place of wanting to stop the followers of Jesus at any cost. They found themselves doing all they could to stop the idea of the Virgin Birth of Christ and His Death and Resurrection by any means possible. Both Josiah and Patrous were aware of the evil that was in the leader's hearts.

Knowing the evil in their hearts, and having had Paul give them an understanding of scripture, they understood why the priests and Pharisees had turned their back on God the Father, because they could not bear to let the control of the people go. Both men knew that the leaders of the Jews were heading for an eternity of destruction, but had no idea what to do to stop where these guys were heading. They just knew these men who led the Jews were the ones that Jesus the Christ was talking about when he stated that it would be better for a millstone to be tied around their neck than cause one of the Father's little ones to stumble.

Josiah walked up to Patrous and said one thing. "Jesus said that it would be better for a man to be to have a millstone tied around his neck and be thrown into the sea than cause one of his little one to stumble.

My friend, they are causing the Father's kids to stumble."

Patrous looked intently at Josiah. "Why is it they want to control other men? Why is it they want to play God? They put so many rules on men that the rules take the place of God the Father. Is it the pride that they have? Is it the same pride Satan had when God the Father kicked him out of Heaven?" Patrous's face started to turn red with anger. "How dare they lead God's kids astray. They know the scriptures, yet the only thing they really want to do is maintain their power. It's not that they don't see Christ as their Messiah. They don't want to give up their power. They can't see what their leading God's people astray means to their eternity or the eternities of the ones they are destroying with their lies?"

Josiah looked directly into the eyes of Patrous. "My friend: Our friend Paul wrote this to the Church. No one can say Jesus is the Christ except by the Holy Spirit of God Himself. Solomon wrote that pride comes before destruction. It's their pride that will keep them from understanding that the Christ is who he says he is. Never forget what Jesus said to us when we saw him walk out of the tomb. 'You are forgiven.' Those are the only three words he spoke to us in an audible voice. We know what we saw. We know what we heard. And we know that the Jews will never believe us. The Jews know we are telling the truth. They will never say Jesus is Lord. The Holy Spirit left the temple the second Jesus died on that Cross that I built. The veil was torn. God's Holy Spirit has walked away from his people. Jesus would become that light to bring light the gentiles."

Josiah heard the light knocking on his door. He turned and walked over to the door, opened it slightly, and saw Anna. He opened the door wide and with a great expression of joy said, "Anna, my dear sweet Anna. How are you?"

Anna looked at him. He could see the anger still in her eyes. She said, "Look, one of your death tree was used to kill not only Jesus, but like I told you before, my brother was also nailed to one. I just need three of your cross necklaces. I have friends who want them."

Josiah turned and walked over to the table with the cross necklaces. He looked at them with a tear in his eye. He realized deep inside himself that what brought the believers in Christ the ultimate victory was bringing about his total defeat with Anna because he had built them. He was coming to realize that even though forgiveness came from God the Father through his Son Jesus because of his victory over death, the one person who he really loved would never be able to share that love with him because of the crosses he built. He picked up three and walked back over to Anna. Handing them to her, he said, "My gift."

The anger welled up in Anna. "I will take nothing from you as a gift." She threw the money down on the table, turned, and stormed out.

An empty feeling hit Josiah in the gut like a sledgehammer.

Patrius walked over and took Josiah in his arms and let him cry like a baby. "My friend, the damage you have done in her heart may be permanent. Our actions do have consequences. We get forgiven by God, but we still have to pay the price for our actions. You chose to make money off of people being put to death. Nailing them to the cross was my choice. We got extra pay for doing it. I have to live with that for the rest of my life. Jesus told us both those three words, "'You are forgiven.' That forgiveness is the ultimate victory, we have to walk in the victory. It's not a battle we win. It is the battle that Christ had won when he walked out of the grave."

*　　*　　*

A short time later,　there was a knock. Josiah set down the cross necklace he was working on and walked over, grabbed the wooden latch and eased the door open. Standing outside was John, the one Jesus called the beloved. The one that Jesus had told from the cross, "Behold your mother," as he spoke of Mary. Josiah opened the door wide.

John walked over to Josiah and embraced him warmly. "I know what you experienced at the tomb. I know of the words that Jesus said to you before he walked off. That is a powerful testimony. I do feel, however, that it is impera-tive that you each understand all of the teaching of Jesus to be able to be used in the kingdom to the fullest. I have been writing for several months the entire history of the ministry of Jesus the Christ. There was one key thing he said that you must understand. The leaders had a hatred for the Christ. A big hatred. They saw him as taking away their power. Yet he continued to love those very people who hated him. Jesus understood the men wanting power. Remember there was a reason he had Solomon write that pride comes before destruction. Remember this. God the Father had Solomon build that great temple. But it is coming down

Jesus stated there will not be one stone left upon another. The reason is this, the pride of their worship is going to be taken from them. They worship power instead of God the Father. They want to control God's people more than they want to lead them into a relationship with Him. Their pride was what they wanted to protect. When Jesus said there would be not one stone left upon another he meant it. When anything comes between a person and their relationship with God the Father through His Son Jesus by His Holy Spirit that thing has to go."

Josiah walked over to John with tears running down his cheeks. "What then can we do as followers of the Christ? If what you say it true, the Pharisees and priests will stop at nothing to get the gospel of Christ stopped. I can't stop what I am doing. I feel that those cross necklaces are what I am supposed to do now, what should I do?" Then like a bolt of lightning it struck him. *It's the crosses. It's all about the Cross of Christ. That's where our redemption comes from. We don't have to play their silly political games, we just have to preach Christ and Him crucified.*

Josiah turned and looked Patrous in the eye. "My friend, we have been going about this wrong. We have been hiding hoping that getting these crosses on people's necks would be all it would take. We have been cowering in these buildings hoping that the big bad priest and Pharisees would leave us alone. That's not what Christ wants of us. He wants us to be talking to people. He wants us interacting with people. He wants us to lead the priests to him. What they do with it is up to God the Father. But we have to try."

"James, Jesus's brother, wrote that our faith must be followed by works or it's dead. Man, I want faith that is alive. If what the Father has me doing with these crosses that hang around people's necks gets me nailed to a cross, then at least I have lived out my faith. I destroyed so much over the years building those 'other' crosses. I had a hand in destroying so many of God's people, to die now helping spread the word would be worth it to me."

Patrous looked at Josiah. "Today I saw John and Peter going up to the temple to pray. They saw a lame man. I heard Peter simply say that he had no money, but what he had he would give him. I heard him tell the guy, 'In the name of Jesus, rise up and walk.' The guy picked up his pallet and walked away. The next thing I saw was the priest going totally nuts. They started screaming. It was the Sabbath. The formerly lame guy was 'working.' I just can't believe how they want to control every part of peoples' lives."

Just then there was a knock at the door. Josiah walked over and saw that it was Peter. As he walked in he smiled at Josiah and Patrous.

"Gentlemen, things are starting to get hot. You're starting to get under the skin of the priests and Pharisees. With those small crosses God has you making, people are starting to ask the believers what they really mean. As the believers are telling them, more and more people are coming to the realization of who Jesus the messiah really is. Then when the temple leaders see that The Father is still moving among his people they freak out even more. They see their power starting to evaporate. They will do anything to keep it. We must keep spreading the word of salvation through Christ. Jesus is going to use everything that we do to touch people who are hurting. But the leaders of the temple see their flock getting smaller and smaller. They must try to stop God. By trying to stop God the Father it will be the ruin of Israel for thousands of years."

Josiah asked, "Then what are you smiling about. This is not going to go well for us, is it?"

Peter gave a nervous chuckle as he said, "It's like what Paul said. We have had some disagreements on small matters. But on this point I agree with him. When he wrote his letter to the Philippians, he told them, 'To live is Christ, to die is gain.' You see, we gain no matter what."

The hour was late. Peter and John said their good-byes as did Patrous. All three men left. With eyes that were watering profusely, Josiah blew out the candles and went to bed. He finally understood. No matter what the future held, he would win because Christ had already won.

15
. . . . . .
Fury in the Temple

I t was five am. Josiah lay quietly in his bed. He could hear the crickets outside his window. He heard the rustle in the grass. He heard the voices of the Temple guard as they approached his home. He knew in his heart this would not be good for him. Yet he lay there waiting.

He heard the door being broken down. He heard the voice of the guard. "Who are you?" he heard a very scared voice.

The voice of Gabriel answered sternly. "You won't hurt God's servant tonight. Go back and tell your priests that if they keep on the path they are following, that as Jesus said, there will not be one stone left on another."

Josiah could hear the grown men crying like babies in his house. He wanted to go into the room and see for himself what was going on, but he knew he should not. He knew these men to be some of the bravest in Israel, yet they were crying like babies. Or worse yet, scared puppies.

The guards went running back to the priests. They told them what they saw. The priests became furious and called them cowards and had them removed from the temple guard service when they heard the message Gabriel had given the guards protecting Josiah and Patrous.

"How can we believe such foolishness?" the chief priest said after the men had left their presence. "How?"

The Pharisees just shook their heads.

But one young man had to ask a question.

"What if they were telling the truth? What if they really saw the huge angel? Would you not react in the same manner?"

One could almost see the steam come out from the priest's ears. "How could you even think such a thing? God wants us here. He would not send an angel to warn us about the path we are on; he ordained it!"

The young man was struck by the Holy Spirit as he said, "Rightly did Paul write to Timothy of you. You take on a form of Godliness but deny its power." He continued, "How dare you. You profane the temple with your lies. You call it a holy place, but you are leading God's people astray every day in it. In Jesus he gave you the ability to be cleansed of your sins. But instead you are choosing to die in them. The problem is you are taking a lot of good people with you."

The priests and Pharisees became enraged. They grabbed the young man and threw him out of the temple into the street. They declared him to be unclean and forbade him to enter the temple again.

The Holy Spirit of God had one more thing for him to say. "This temple you call holy stopped being holy when the veil was torn. The Holy Spirit left. Rightly did Jesus say this building will be torn down and not one stone will be left on another."

The young man turned and left. As he did the high priest nodded to the guard who followed him out in the courtyard and killed him through with his sword.

Peter walked up to the young man. Touched him and said, "In the name of Jesus Christ be healed." Instantly the bleeding stopped.

The young man got up, walked over to the guard, and said, "I forgive you."

The look on the guard's face surprised all around him. He looked at his sword and it still had the young man's blood on it. He looked at the young man standing across from him. He shook his head and walked back into the temple.

He walked up to the priest and showed him his sword. The priest got a look of disgust on his face. "I did not tell you to kill him!" he shouted.

The anger on the guard's face was evident. "How dare you try that garbage on me! I did exactly what you commanded me. You told me when you nodded I was supposed to 'take care of him,' yet you claim you did not want him dead. You call yourself a priest and break one of the Ten Commandments that Moses got from God himself." He then walked across the room. "By the way, after I ran him through, after the sword went in his back and out his front, Peter touched him. Spoke healing in Jesus's name. The bleeding stopped. He got up, walked across the courtyard where I was standing, and said those three words to me. 'I forgive you.'" He stormed out of the temple and as he left the temple gate he wiped the dust from his feet.

As he walked out of the gate, the guard turned white as he looked at Peter, then the man whom he had tried to kill, and then back to Peter. "What must I do to be saved?" he asked with a quivering voice.

Peter looked at him with compassion. "There is only one name under heaven by which a man can be saved. That is the name of Jesus Christ. Repent, receive Christ as your Lord and Savior and be baptized and you will be saved."

Josiah looked at the men. He saw the tough guard melt like snow on a hot July day. He saw more rage on the face of the priest than ever. He saw the man who had been run through leaping and laughing with a newfound joy. He knew one thing. Every time something like this happens, the priests become more enraged. They saw their power slipping away. They saw more and more people being drawn to the Christ. He looked to his right. There was Anna. She realized Josiah had seen her and quickly blended into the crowd.

Josiah looked to heaven and prayed one quick prayer. "Father, will Anna ever be able to forgive me?"

It was as if the Father of all and his Son Jesus answered his prayer with just a couple of words. "In time, my son, in time."

Josiah got his head back into the task at hand. He put his arm around the man who had been killed and walked him to a safe location. He did not want to have to see him resurrected again that day.

* * *

Back in the temple, the uproar was deafening. The chief priest was storming around the temple screaming and asking how to stop this thing that was going on. "People raised from the dead? Nonsense. We can't accept what they say Jesus was about. There is no way we will survive that. Our power is gone if we do. If we give in and say that *may* have been the messiah, then they will ask us why we had him killed? Just so he could walk out of the grave."

A young man walked up to the priest. He seemed to come from nowhere. Dressed totally in white, he walked directly to the priest and looked him squarely in the eye. "If you keep on the road you are currently following, you are going to put your people into a position of losing God's land. They will be scattered all over the world for two thousand years. Your deception of them, they will take as truth. Jesus said, 'I am the way the truth and the life, no one comes to the Father but by me.' Your punishment will go on forever. You still have time to change."

He turned and walked away. The priest in his anger turned for just a second to keep from attacking him. He turned back and the young man was gone. He started to walk. His thoughts were going wild. He asked himself, *How can Jewish beliefs survive if we accept Jesus for who he may have may have been? How do we make this work?* He turned again and the young man was standing there.

"You question God Almighty. You think he could not make it all work. Don't reject His Son. Don't lead His people astray. He sent his promised Messiah. Accept the forgiveness that is being offered through him. Without the blood of Christ there is no forgiveness."

The priest's anger could be seen in the redness of his face. Deep in his heart he knew he would not give in. He could not believe that after all these years of service God would reject him for not letting God's Son Jesus be his messiah. Would God really send him to hell for not believing in Jesus?

He turned back and the priest who was standing there. "The answer to your question is this. God sent His Son Jesus. Even though you had him killed, God the Father brought him back to life. If you reject that you have no hope. You have a choice. You can try to hold onto your power here on earth and lose it, and be sent to hell because of that choice. Or you can lead God's people to His Son and see them set free. The choice is yours."

The priest turned and walked back to his quarters. He knew in his heart what he would do. He could not give up the praise and adulation of men for God's praise. He would continue to lead the people away from the Christ. And would continue walking toward the destruction of himself and Israel.

He ordered Josiah into his chambers. When he was brought in, the chief priest walked up to him and went nose to nose.

"Listen, you spit of a camel, if you keep doing what you are doing with these necklaces, I am going to have you nailed to a cross. You need to stop spreading your filthy lies about this Jesus walking out of the tomb."

Josiah, not backing off from the nose to nose position that the priest had put him into said, "Look, you whitewashed tomb, you know the truth, yet you keep your people from the salvation that God the Father through His Son by His Holy Spirit is offering them. Jesus told you that there would not be one stone left upon another. If you don't stop this, you will see this building brought to nothing. Unless you repent and turn to the living Christ, your power on this earth is short, and your eternity in Hell will last a very, very long time."

The priest's face turned red with anger. "How dare you speak to me in that tone of voice. I am the high priest of God."

Before he could say anything else, Josiah spoke up, "Not anymore. That ended the second the veil was torn in the Holy of Holies. The Holy Spirit left the temple.
God the Father through His Son by His Holy Spirit will restore His Nation and the people will be brought back into fellowship with him through His Son, but your time in hell, will be long, and never ending. One
other thing. I was there. I saw him walk out of the grave. I saw the powerful flash behind the rock. I saw the rock roll away. Jesus is alive."

The anger from the high priest exploded. He commanded the guards to throw him out. He turned and went back into his chambers. The one thing he did not expect was his wife of thirty-five years to be standing there. "Listen, my husband, I get a feeling that if you continue on this path it will not go well for you or for this country. If what Josiah said is true, you are not fighting against a man, you are fighting against God himself. You will lose this battle."

In his anger he struck his wife, knocking her to the floor. As he looked on her struggling to get up, the shame of his pride struck him like a heard of bulls stampeding in anger. "I am so sorry; I am a fool. Jesus was not God. He is dead. I will not have the Hebrew faith destroyed because of a charlatan."

His wife looked at her husband. she put her hand to the cheek that took his blow, and walked into their bedchamber, shut the door and cried. "*I know Jesus is who he says he is. Mary is a friend of mine. She sat at his feet. She took her life savings for the ointment that he wiped on his feet with her hair. I know my husband is wrong and will lead his people to their own destruction. God is there anything I can do to change his mind. I know Jesus said it would be better for a mill stone to be tied around his neck and thrown into the sea than cause one of your little ones to stumble. He is causing a whole nation to stumble. What can I do?*" she prayed.

At this point the Holy Spirit started to have conversation with her. She walked to the room where the priest kept his personal wealth. She looked at the thousands and thousands of silver coins. The spirit spoke to her telling her that the people had sacrificed of their own beings to raise the money for God's work.
The only problem was that money was not going to the work for which it was intended. She looked to heaven. She walked over to the money bags and took one hundred pieces of silver and put it into another pouch. She knew what she had to do, and she was about to do it.

* * *

The guards threw Josiah out of the temple. They threw him so hard he ended up a pile in the dirt. As he picked himself up, he could hear a guard warning him.

"You better quit all this Jesus stuff if you know what's good for you!"

It was as if someone else was speaking to him. "It's time to double down." He got up, smiled to himself, and thought, *Yup, it's time to double down.*

16
· · · · · ·
It's Time to Double Down

As Josiah walked into his work shop, he looked around, all was quiet. He walked across the room lifting his hands toward heaven and prayed one prayer. "Father, how do I double what you have me do making these necklaces and give them away at no cost?" He walked around the room continuing in prayer. Then he heard a pounding at the door. His thoughts raced. *Would he take a beating at the hands of the guards?*

He walked over and peaked out the crack in the door. Standing on the other side was the high priest's wife. He opened the door slowly and invited her in.

"Josiah, my husband is more worried about his position than the salvation of God's people or the destruction of Israel itself. He does not believe that Rome would destroy the temple. But you and I both know that is not correct. It will happen and our people will be spread all over the world. You have a short period of time. You must double your efforts to get as many people 'born again' as possible.

I was there when Jesus talked to Nicodemus and told him he must be born again. I have accepted Jesus as my savior and have been baptized quietly. I have been born again. I have brought with me one hundred pieces of silver. I want you to make as many of these cross necklaces as you can. I want you talking to as many people as you can and lead them to the Christ. After they get saved, I want you to give them one of these necklaces. We must be able to tell who is a believer and who is not. I want you to charge them nothing. But you must say nothing to my husband. If he finds out, he will have me stoned."

Josiah reached out and took the money from her hand. He smiled as he walked over to touch her shoulder and said, "Thank you. I will follow the instruction our Father through His Son by His Spirit used you to give me. Thank you again. I do think you should leave now, for you own protection." She smiled and walked to the door, letting herself out.

Walking into her chambers, her priest husband was standing there waiting for her. "Where have you been, woman?"

She knew she could not lie. But at the same time she was not in any big hurry to tell her enraged husband where she had been. She decided to tell him exactly what she had done. If she would get sent to be with Jesus she knew it would be worth it. In a trembling voice she told him the truth. "I went into the money storage bin and picked out one hundred pieces of silver.

I took that money to Josiah and handed it to him. I told him I wanted him to use that money to make as many cross necklaces as he could, and give them to the people who have accepted the salvation that the Christ is offering."

His red-faced rage caught her off guard. "How can you believe that he is still alive? I saw him die on the cross. They say that he is alive. Where is he? I don't see him."

Fearlessly she walked over to the priest, stood nose to nose with him and said, "You are not telling the truth. Jesus did walk out of the grave. You know it and so do I. The only reason you deny it is to keep your position of power and prestige. If you admitted how you falsely accused Jesus so you could have the Romans nail him to a cross the Jewish leaders would drive you out of the temple."

"Liar!" he screamed. "Jesus and his disciples were nothing but con men. They should all be nailed to crosses!"

Tears started coming to his wife of years and years. "How can you say that? You know the truth, yet you deny it. Do you realize what you are doing? For God so loved the world that he gave his son. You cannot deny what Isaiah said. That one must be raised up for the nation. What I cannot understand is this: All your life you have been saying you're serving God. God sends his son. You reject his messiah. Why?"

The high priest, who knew she was telling the truth, said. "I cannot accept Jesus as God's son. If I do all my power is lost. I will be seen as the one who killed God's son. I feel like I am trapped. I must follow through on this. Josiah must die."

*   *   *

Back at Josiah's house he was starting to work at a fever-ish pace making the cross necklaces. He knew very well that his time on this earth was growing shorter by the day. Several of the disciples had been killed, and Paul was in the Roman prison waiting the Roman ruler's sentence. Josiah knew that his time was short. He had no idea at this point in history what his fate would be. He just knew that he had to continue spreading the word the best he could. By candlelight at night he would make the crosses. During the day he would be out talking to people. He led person after person to that saving prayer. Person after person was baptized into the Christ and his kingdom. As a result, he would see people's whole lives changed in an instant.

One hot afternoon he saw a young lady crying in the street. She was sitting, legs crossed in the hot sun. As he stood over her, she looked up at him and asked one simple question. "Can you help me?"

He reached down and touched her shoulder.

She looked up at him with her big brown eyes and smiled.

Josiah asked her one question. "What can I do for you?"

Tears running down her cheeks she had trouble keep-ing from crying. "My parents have sent me away. I am a believer in the Christ of God. They do not want to be sent out of the temple, so they sent me away."

Suddenly he heard the sweet voice of Anna. "Josiah, is there something I can help with here?"

Josiah turned and saw the young lady he loved. He started to speak, but Anna stopped him. "Josiah, don't even think that I am here for you. I am here to help this young lady. The Holy Spirit sent me here to help this young lady. Gabriel was at my bedside when I woke this morning and told me to come here. I will handle this, you can leave."

Josiah shrugged his shoulders and walked away. The rest of the day was spent sharing Jesus with as many people he came in contact with as possible. He told the story over and over again about building the crosses and being at the tomb when Jesus came back to life. People were coming to a saving knowledge of Christ in droves. The leaders of the temple were seeing their captive flock being taken from them. Josiah could see his time was short. The urgency in his sharing the Christ continued to increase each day. He knew he could not let himself get distracted by everything else going on around him. All he knew was that with everyone he talked to there seemed to be an urgency he did not understand, yet he did. He seemed to know deep down this his time was short to share the truth of Jesus the Christ with the multitudes.

He walked every street, knocked on doors, and talked to as many people as he could about who Jesus is. He told the story over and over again how he and Patrous were there when Jesus rose from the dead, and walked out of the tomb. He told people about hearing the words "You are forgiven" from Jesus. He found himself leading people in prayer over and over again. Every time he would look at the priests they seemed to be red in the face with anger.

He saw them walk into Pilate's quarters. He knew that was not a good thing. Totally exhausted, he headed back to his home.

That night he made himself a lamb dinner with all the trimmings. He had John and Patrous join him for the celebration of his day. They drank a cup of wine and enjoyed the lamb. There was a quiet, however. They could sense something was not right. It was like there was a gloom in the air. Nothing seemed just right.

After everyone left it was time to sleep. But sleep would not come. It was as if the power of the priests would have its way. He was to find out just how ruthless the priests were to hold onto their power over the people. He had distributed all of the crosses he was able to make with the silver the Priest wife had given him. But he lay in bed tossing and turning not being able to sleep. He sensed it. He knew that all the power of Satan would be unleashed to stop the spread of the good news of Christ Jesus. He knew he had done his best with the time he had. And he knew he was forgiven. He prayed for rest. And sleep came.

The next morning, he left his home and walked outside. The air was fresh, yet something did not seem right. It was as though his world was about to crash around him, he did not quite understand it, yet he did. He had been making many enemies among the priesthood for the last few years. The cross necklaces he had been making were making their way around believers' necks. People had been accepting the Christ and his salvation, the more people received God's salvation through his Son by his Spirit, the madder the priesthood became as they saw their power over the people become less and less

Then one morning it happened just as it had the morning they broke into Josiah's house demanding the cross for the Christ. But this day would be one in which Josiah would spend with his friends. It would be a day of fulfillment and enjoyment. They would sit and listen to John's teachings on love and the compassion of Christ, and how important it was to have that love in their lives so they could share it with others. Just as the soldiers were the beginning of a newness in his life, albeit a violent start, this day would be a gentle yet fulfilling, relaxing time of freshness with his closest friends.

As Josiah sat and listened to John, he noticed Anna across the way. He started to get up to walk over to her. She saw him, shook her head slightly, and turned away. Josiah stopped cold in his tracks. At the end of the study he did not want to leave. It was as though this would be his last study. This would be the last time he would ever see his brothers and sisters in Christ. He did not understand it at that time, but knew somehow he would soon. Finally very late that night he left and went back to his home.

17
. . . . . .
Hosanna

The next day John was to visit again. The message
he had would shake both Josiah and Patrous to
core. He knocked at the door.

"Why, hello, John," was the greeting John received
from Josiah.

"My friend, we both know that you made the cross and
Patrous over there nailed him to the cross he was killed
on. The one that was used for Christ to be the savior of
the world. But do you realize the dynamics that God had to
arrange for that to happen?"

"What do you mean?" Patrous asked.

John looked at the two with an urgency on his face. "It's
like this. At the fall God started to put things in motion
for the salvation of the world. God the Father looked at
His People and wanted to have that intimate relationship
which he had created them for. Adam and Eve both
started to walk away from that. Father purposed in His
mind to cleanse man from his sin. He also knew that
because of man's choice, there was no good in them.

He knew there was only one way that level of purification could take place, and that was to make the sacrifice himself. He could also see that man would not receive what he was going to do for them unless they understood what the level of their sin was. Our Father knew that He could just force it, but that would not be the best. That would be forcing them to love Him. He created truth and he knew the truth was that without choice love would not exist."

John continued, "God started to put in motion at that point in history man's being reunited with him. He had to have everything perfect. The times had to be such that the Jews would be desperate for a savior. He had to have the perfect mother created for Jesus. That would be Mary. All one has to do is read the writing of the prophets and see what was going to happen. All one would have to do is read the history of Israel and understand the process that was needed for everything to be perfect.

"So what we had at the time that Jesus the Christ entered Jerusalem was the perfect storm. The Jewish people were desperate for a messiah. They were shouting Hosanna to the Son of David. For you, Patrous, who may not be familiar with that word, it means, "save us, please." Jesus had just raised Lazarus from the dead. But what they did not understand was what the Kingdom of God was."

Josiah got a confused look on his face.

John continued to speak. "Jesus taught a great deal on the Kingdom of God. When he stood before Pilate he was asked if he was King of the Jews. He honestly said he was. But he also said that His Kingdom was not of this world. That's what threw off the people who wanted to be out from under Roman oppression. When they saw he was not going to set up a new Jewish kingdom they deserted him. When the Pharisees started yelling, Crucify Him they joined in. They went as far as to say let his blood be on us and our children. They wanted a Messiah, but not the kind God the Father intended. But God's Son Jesus is the Messiah. Remember what Jesus said. 'For God so loved the world that He gave His Only Son. That whoever believes should not perish but have everlasting life.' He was speaking of Himself. He is God's only begotten Son. God the Father took the time needed for the perfect mom for the Christ to be born to. Mary was that woman."

Josiah stroked his beard as he said, "There's a whole lot more to this than what I thought. Even those few moments you spent explaining all that really had to take place, but that still does not answer my question as to why God let me build those death trees."

John looked at Josiah and answered quite wisely. "It's not that God let you do anything. It's your greed that drove you to be a tool of the Romans to kill Jews. If you had not repented of what you were doing, and received Christ as your savior, he had a special place in hell for you. You were used as an instrument to kill God chosen people. You allowed yourself to be used by the enemy for his purpose. But Christ redeemed you. All I can say is you better walk in that redemption for the rest of your life."

With that he turned and faced Patrous. "And you, my friend, you nailed him to the cross. You were used as a tool of the Romans as well. You did your job. You were forgiven at the tomb as well. Remember to walk in it. You both have a testimony that needs to be shared. You both now have an understanding of some of what happened historically. You have to start moving outside of this box you are living in. The people need to hear about Jesus. Your time here is short. You need to use every minute wisely. Remember this. The moments you spend telling someone about what Jesus the Christ did for them have eternal value. Both for you and for them. There is nothing more important that you can do with your time than see a person's eternity changed. There are so many things we can do with the time we have here that has eternal value. The finite really does effect on the infinite. Every waking minute that you have on this earth must be used in a way that will have a direct effect on someone's eternity."

Josiah walked over to his work table. He picked up one of the small crosses he had been working on. Picked it up and tossed it in John's direction as he asked him, "John, does that mean I am wasting time making these mini crosses that believers wear around their necks? That time could be spent out talking to more people about the Christ?"

John took the cross between his fingers. He turned it so he could look at it from many different angles. He held it up to the light. He turned and looked at Josiah and simply said, "What you have here is something that gets people asking questions. Those questions have been leading to people receiving Christ as their lord." He continued," The chief priests and the elders have one thing in mind. That is to stop the spread of the Jewish people being saved by the blood of Christ and walking in the freedom that offers.

They were there when the veil was torn. They know that the Holy Spirit left the temple at that very second. But if they lose the people they lose their power. When they lose their power they lose all control. When they lose control they lose everything."

Josiah got a puzzled look on his face as he said, "What you're telling me is this:God sends His Son to save his people from their sins. If the priests and elders receive Him not only is Israel saved from their sins but the people individually are saved as well. Israel the nation would have been redeemed. But they are rejecting the very savior that God the Father sent to redeem mankind. Because they are rejecting Him, He leaves the temple and will dwell in the hearts and minds of people. Men and women become the dwelling place of His Spirit, thereby making the hearts of men and women who receive his salvation the Holy of Holies instead. Mankind becomes God's Holy Temple, is that correct?"

John smiled as he said, "I was there in the Garden after His last supper. I heard Him ask the Father that as the Spirit of God Himself dwelt in Him that the same Sprit would dwell in man in the same manner. That's what happened when the veil was torn in a perfect manner from top to bottom the second Jesus the Christ died on the Cross. Forty days after he ascended to heaven the Holy Spirit came on all of those people standing there as Peter preached. There were flames over each head there. Men, women, and children all had the same flame over their head as proof of the power that was starting to indwell all of them."

John turned and looked into the outer darkness as the hour grew late. "Jesus said that there will not be one stone left on another. Believe me, there won't. I don't know how it is going to happen, but it will. It won't be long now. God the Father has pulled his presence out of Israel. The leaders will try to maintain control of the people. This will cause the Jews are going to be in exile for thousands of years, and it's because the chief priest and elders of the nation rejected the Messiah that God Himself sent. Jesus once said don't fear him who can kill the body and after words do nothing. But rather fear him who after he kills the body can cast your soul into hell. Because the Jews no long fear God, they are going to be taught a lesson. When they start to trust, their land will be restored."

Josiah looked directly into John's eyes as he responded. "Okay then, my friend. What is the real power of the cross? I built well over a hundred of them and there was nothing really exciting about them. Two logs squared up to withstand a man fighting for his life."

John was blunt. "The power is in the resurrection. The power comes from Christ Jesus being killed on one, and walking out of the grave. Christ's cross killed his body once. That body, as you saw, rose and walked out of the grave."

Josiah looked over at Patrous who had been listening. "We both saw him walk out of that tomb. Just before it happened the light flashing behind the rock was amazing. I have never seen anything like it before or after. The colors of the flashes were nothing short of spectacular."

John looked over at the two and continued what he was saying. "I was in the locked room when Christ walked in.

He showed us his hands and his side, then he told us to go tell the world what we saw. All three of us have seen the risen Christ. We now have to go out and tell the world. Josiah, you must keep making those crosses."

"But you have to do one more thing. You have to keep talking. You have to get out there and tell folks what you saw. You just explained to me the colors of the explosion of life when Christ returned to his body. The energy at that point in time must have been tremendous. You need to start talking to everyone you come in contact with. If you can shout it from corners or house tops, do it."

"Expect resistance. Expect the powers of hell to try to stop you. The priests and elders who once called them-selves friends with God are now his enemies. Don't get me wrong. I am a Jew. God the Father through His Son by His Spirit loves the Jews, his people. But the leaders of His people are now leading His people astray. I really would not want to be in their position on judgment day. Remember what Jesus said. He was talking about children at the time. But God has a bunch of children. Those people are put as shepherds over the people. They had the prophecies that were fulfilled. They knew them backward and forward. He said it would be better for a millstone to be tied around their neck and thrown into the sea than to cause one of those little ones to stumble. Believe me, they will wish they had never been born the day they stand in front of Christ when he sits on the judgment seat."

"Keep this in mind. The people who receive Christ at your word will be grateful to you for sharing Jesus Christ with them. But the leaders of the Jews will hate you and set and set out to kill you.

Remember they care nothing for the people except for the power they have over them. When they saw the people on the side of the road shouting hosanna to the son of David they were shouting save us please."

"The leaders of the Jews only saw their power being taken from them. Their jealousy will end up destroying the land of Israel for two thousand years. I just know it did not have to be that way. God loves Israel. I just wish they really loved him."

Josiah and Patrous looked at each other. Patrous simply said, "Looks to me like it's time we go outside of these walls and start to shout and tell people what we saw."

Josiah only had a couple of things to say. "Paul is out there making tents to support what God is having him do. I will take the crosses that people can wear around their neck to support what God is calling us to. This has to be handled with care. Remember Jesus threw the money changer out of the temple. We don't want to fall into that category. But this I do know. It's time to get to work. People have to know what God the Father through the Son by the Spirit has done for them. It's up to us to tell them."

With that they both turned in. Tomorrow would be the first day of an adventure that would change men's and women's hearts forever.

18
· · · · · ·
Where the Lord Places His Name

T he next morning Josiah would wake like he did every morning. He looked at the scroll sitting on his table. He unrolled it and came to Exodus 20:24. "Every place I cause my name to be remembered, I will come to you and bless you."

Then he thought of all the little crosses he was making. His mind would go back to the crosses he made that killed people, then he looked at the small one with a leather strap through the top. That cross was going to save people. They would see it not as the cruel cross used to kill freedom fighters, but as a tool of redemption that the Christ would overcome. The cross he was nailed to killed his body only for a short time. Josiah and Patrous had seen the risen Christ walk out of the tomb in total victory.

His mind went back to the fireworks that seemed to go off in the tomb. He remembered the light show from behind the rock as life came back to the body of Jesus the Christ. He smiled. Then he turned and walked across his room. He realized that the crosses he was making were the very tools that would be used to have Christ's name remembered, and by doing so have the people be blessed.

The one thing he could not shake was that the leaders of the Jews hated him. They really did not want the name of Christ remembered. They would just as soon have that name forgotten from history. They did not want their power stripped from them. The thought if they were to acknowledge Christ that their power would be lost forever. In his heart he knew that unless they received the Christ as their savior they would be cast into the outer darkness where there would be gnashing of teeth.

He heard a knock at the door. He walked over and opened it. He looked outside and it was John.

"My brother, You look terrible. What happened?" "I just found out they have Paul. They carted him off to Rome. He asked to be judged by Rome. Josiah, I think there could be some real trouble for him. I do know this. God our Father through His Son Jesus the Christ can be trusted. As we trust the worry stops," John stated in a hopeful tone.

"John, what about you? It seems to me that the Jewish leaders are out to silence all of us who are walking with Jesus. Look, both Patrous and myself saw the bright lights going off behind the stone. We both heard him say 'You are forgiven.' We both know what we saw."

John looked at him and asked one question. "Have you been baptized since you have believed?"

"Yes, but to be honest, my understanding is still a bit unclear. We have baptized a great many people because that was the Lord's command. I am just not real clear on why he commanded it."

John smiled a bit. "Some things are a bit of mystery. I think it has to do with the Lord putting his name on us. In Exodus we are told that where the Lord puts his name, those who have it placed on will be blessed. It's a brand if you will. Much like is done to cattle. It's an outward sign of inward obedience."

Josiah stood looking at John for a few moments. Both men were silent as Josiah was drinking it all in. Just then Patrous spoke. "My compatriot Cornelius was baptized with his whole family. From the youngest to the oldest child. And he has a bunch little ones. He is committed to raising all of his children in the way."

Josiah looked at John. "Can a child believe so that he can be baptized?"

John shrugged his shoulders. "Jesus said, 'Suffer the children to come onto me. Do not forbid them. For such is the kingdom of God.' That's what the Master said." He got up out of his chair and walked across the room. "You suppose I could get enough of these little crosses for each of Cornelius's children?"

"Look, guys, the leaders of the tabernacle are scared. They know who Jesus is who he says he is. They know that he walked out of the tomb. That's why they bribed the guards. Their fear is that if they say to the folks that Jesus really was the Messiah they will be destroyed by the people. They know that the people followed him. They also know that the people will know that they were totally manipulated when the Christ was sent to the cross by Pilate. They have painted themselves into a corner that they cannot get out of. What they have to do is try to destroy anything before it gets started. What they are finding is that they are not fighting to stop us, they are fighting to stop God himself," John stated with full authority.

Josiah walked over to his work table. He picked up a rough cut of a cross that he was preparing to be worn around someone's neck. He held it up to the light. He could almost see a blood stain on it. He knew that blood shed was an awful price so those who truly placed their trust in God the Father through Christ his Son by his Holy Spirit would be able to walk in newness of life. He thought to himself, "*I can see only a brief period of time. The name of Christ is changing everything. We are to look for his return. I wonder what these all will look like years down the line. I wonder...*"

Patrous looked over at him. "What is going through your mind, my friend?"

Josiah was just about to say, "Oh nothing." He caught himself. "I think that this fraud the Jewish leaders are placing on their followers is going to become imbedded in the minds of the Jews for centuries to come. They are going to ignore the prophets of the past. Everything they uttered pointed to the Christ. They knew in their hearts that Jesus is who he said he was. But they are going to pass their lies onto the generations to come."

Patrous simply said a few words. "Let's go for a walk." And headed for the door. Josiah and John followed close behind him.

Josiah said. "How could the leaders lie to the people? It seems people will do anything to stay in their position of influence and power. What I don't understand is why they are so concerned about their position and not the people's eternity. Jesus bled and died and walked out of the grave. The prophets spoke of this. The longer it goes the more it festers. This is a lie that will go on for centuries."

Just then they found themselves surrounded by the temple guards. "What gives you the right to challenge the priests?" the captain of the guard demanded.

Patrous went toe to toe with the head guard. The guard could feel his breath on his face he was so close. "The Lord Jesus Christ. Your law says one should not bear false witness. Yet you're denying the Christ, which means you're doing exactly that. How dare they lie to God's people."

"What do you know about the law? You uncircumcised gentile," the guard responded.

"I know what I saw. I was at the tomb. I saw the Christ walk out of the tomb and stand as close to me as I am to you," Patrous said.

The guard's face started to turn beet red with anger. "You know our law requires two witnesses. Who is your other?" he demanded."

Josiah spoke up. "That would be me. How can you take the high priest's side in this? You were standing there when the veil was torn the second Jesus died on the cross. You came running out and told the priests. You know that was the time God himself left the temple. That was the time man became pure so the Holy Spirit could dwell in men's hearts.

How can you let your people not have access the forgiveness that the Christ offers?"

The tension went out of the guard's face. His shoulders relaxed. He bowed his head and the tears started to drip on the ground. "What do I do know? If I go against the high priest, they can have me killed. If I stay with them I am helping people get into hell. God sent His Son to the Jews first. Jesus said, 'I am the way the truth and the life. No one comes to the Father but through Him.' If there is no other way to God's kingdom, then what the leaders of the temple are doing is leading those people to an eternal separation from God the Father. That leaves people with hell. Not a pleasant thought."

Josiah walked over to the guard, put his hands on his shoulder, and prayed for him. "Father, take this man and use him. Walk him into the ministry that you have chosen for him. Have him be the man you have created him to be. Flood his heart with your Holy Spirit so he will have your courage to accomplish all that you have set for him to do. In Jesus's name, amen." He then looked at the guard and asked a simple question. "Would you like to receive the forgiveness that God the Father is offering through His Son the Christ?" The temple Guard, crying, said yes. Josiah led him in a prayer that put the Father's name on him forever.

19

. . . . . .

The First Beating

It was four a.m. Josiah had been working hard the day before. He had spent the day being used by the Father though His Son Jesus by the Holy Spirit to touch many people by sharing the story of the sacrifice that Jesus the Christ made for them. Suddenly, without warning, the door of his home was smashed open and the temple guard stormed in. They stormed in and grabbed Josiah. After grabbing him they would tie him up like a dead pig. They ran a pole through the ties on his hands and feet and carried him to the high priest hanging like a pig that was set to be cooked.

They carried him in to the priests who were sitting there with all their garments looking important. The guards dropped him on the hard stone floor of the temple. The priests walked over to him looking down on him with a look of disdain, yet glee over having the man who now builds crosses for the people.

"We have you now. You can be released with a mere promise to stop the nonsense with all these crosses," the chief priest spoke in somewhat of a seductive tone. He then motioned for Josiah to be untied.

Standing up, Josiah arched his back, as he tried to recover quickly from being dropped on the hard stone floor. He looked at the priest with anger in his eyes. He looked on the face of one who claimed to understand the Law of Moses. Josiah, from all of his experience with Paul, knew they really did not have a clue. "You expect me to walk away from that which I know to be true! You expect me to deny what I saw at the tomb. You expect me to let you lead God's people to being separated from God their Father forever so you can hold onto your power over them for a few measly years? You expect me to deny the living Christ? Rightly did the Christ speak of you when he called you white washed sepulchers. You care more about your power for a season, than the eternity of the people of God in your trust!"

Before he could say anything else, the guard smashed Josiah's mouth with his fist.

"You will not speak to the high priest in those tones," the guard said.

Josiah looked at the guard as he said, "You are as guilty as he is for what is going to happen to God's people. Jesus said that these walls will be torn down. You watch. It is not far off!"

The guard then punched him in the stomach with a blow that would have killed some men. Josiah dropped to his knees and vomited on the floor of the temple. He struggled to his feet and looked at the chief priest. He heard the words.

"Get out, you pig. If you don't stop what you're doing, we will have the Romans nail you to one of the crosses."

Josiah walked out bent over from the blow of the guard. As he stepped onto the street, Anna walked up to him. "Josiah, what happened?"

Josiah proceeded to describe the events of the morning. Then instead of getting sympathy from Anna, he heard anger and almost a gloating in her next chosen few words.

"You had the beating coming. You sold out your people and killed our freedom fighters for silver. You had it coming!" Anna then turned as walked away with just a trace of a smile. As she walked along, however, she remembered the words of the Christ and the prayer that he taught his disciples. "Forgive us as we have forgiven." These words echoed through her mind over and over again. The guilt over what she was feeling struck her to the core. She knew she had not lived to what Christ had taught. Her stomach sank as she thought about what she had just done. She turned hoping to see Josiah and ask for his forgiveness, but he was gone.

Josiah, walking, almost stumbling along, looked up. Patrous was walking right toward him. "My friend, what happened?" he asked.

Josiah, still bent over from the punch, told him the events of the day. Patrous shook his head and asked him, "My friend! What is your game plan now? You know what will happen if you keep building the crosses the believers wear around their neck, don't you?"

Josiah chuckled through his continued pain. "Yes, I do. Let's build more crosses. God our Father knew the day we were conceived the day we will be coming back to him. We have to work while it is day. Let's get to work." With that Josiah suddenly started to feel better. He straightened himself and walked back to his home. He looked and saw a figure sitting next to his door. He asked himself, *Is that Anna?* He then realized it was. He ran through his pain to the house.

She saw him coming. "Josiah, I have to apologize for the way I acted toward you. I was wrong. I have to forgive you for what you have done. I just can't. Please forgive me for not being able to forgive you." With that she turned and walked away from him.

"Wait, please, wait!" Josiah called. *If only I could get a few minutes to speak with her. She has got to understand that forgiveness is something we can let the Father through the Son by His Holy spirit do through us. Lord, please have her find it in her heart to forgive me. It is the best for her. I did what she knows that I did, and there is nothing I can do about that. But by not forgiving me she is hurting herself.*

Once again Josiah felt like he had been hit in the stomach. He dropped to his knees. "God, why? Why can't I just have that relationship with her work?" he prayed and yelled. He got up and turned and there was Peter.

"It could have something to do with you building the cross that her brother was killed on. You helped kill her brother. That's a hard thing to forgive. She looks at you standing here and it's as though you got away with the murder of her brother," Peter continued. "Josiah, you don't realize the damage you have done. For every cross you built families were destroyed. Brothers and sisters of the freedom fighters were forced to see their siblings killed to satisfy the Roman's blood lust. That day Jesus walked out of the grave and told you that you were forgiven means God the Father through the Son by his Holy Spirit will not hold your sin against you. The families you destroyed, the children you left fatherless, do not find it easy to not hold against you what you have done to them. For every freedom fighter that you provided the cross for, there was a family that you put a huge hole in when you supplied the cross that killed their son, brother, uncle, or friend. You have done a lot of damage. To be honest, I would find it hard to forgive you myself."

Josiah was standing there looking at Peter. His lips started to tremble. Tears started to run down his cheeks. His heart started beating fast as he began to sob uncontrollably. "What can I do?" he asked Peter through the tears.

Peter looked intently and directly into the eyes of Josiah as he said, "Jesus, when he spoke to the Pharisees when they came for baptism, told them to show fruits of their repentance. I think it's time you double your efforts to do just that. We are each given only so much time on this earth. We have to live every moment to accomplish as much as we can for God's kingdom. You have some time left on this earth. I encourage you to spend every wak-ing hour working to see the Father's kingdom built for his glory."

Josiah shook his head. "Peter, Patrous and I were there when Christ walked out of the grave. His only words to us were 'You are forgiven.' How can we not spend every waking hour spreading the good news that Christ is risen?

That's why I make those crosses you see more and more believers wearing around their necks. That's why I am taking so much heat from the priests. You know as well as I do they have their captive flock and they don't want to see Christ set them free from the bondage they have them in. Christ made it clear that God the Father will always love his people. But he hates what the Jewish Leaders have done to his people." He turned and walked across the room and picked up a handful of the small crosses. "You see these, Peter? I know what they will lead to. But I am not afraid to die. God's people have to be set free from all of their sins. He has provided the sacrifice in his Son. I have to proclaim it."

Peter answered. "If people could only understand what we witnessed. Jesus did not come into the world to condemn it, but that the world could be saved through him. He also said that God so loved the world that he sent his only Son, so that anyone who believes in Him can be saved. The key to the whole thing is there must be belief. There must be faith. Without faith it is not possible to please God. Faith requires action. We have to tell more and more people about who Jesus Christ really is. As more and more people meet the living Christ they will be drawn away from the lies that the Pharisee and priests are telling them. We must be ready for whatever Satan is going to throw at us through them."

Josiah got up and struggled to cross the room. The beating that the temple guard had given him was taking its toll. He knew, however, that he could not quit making the crosses. He would get up, cross the room and pray with every step that he took His prayer was that he would continue doing things that would strengthen people's faith for the rest of his days on the earth. He then walked across the room. He looked out in the dark and whispered one last prayer.

"Father, wherever Anna is tonight. Watch out for her. Protect her. And give her a heart of forgiveness toward me. In Jesus name. Amen."

20

Anger in the Temple

T he high priest tore his robe. Golden studs were all
over the floor of the temple. "That Josiah has to be
stopped. He claims he was an eyewitness to Jesus walking
out of the grave. That Patrous does not help. He 'claims' to
have been there with him. Shoot! He nailed the Christ to
that cross. Now he is claiming that he too saw Jesus walk
out of the tomb. The veil of the temple being ripped in
two the second Jesus died. The disciples claimed the Holy
Spirit left the temple at that second. If this keeps going,
every Jew in Israel will follow them. Our power will be
stopped. We know that Jesus fulfilled every prophecy, so
are we going against God himself? If we are God will
fulfill what Jesus said about the temple. Not one stone
will be left upon another. God is the ultimate power. If
Jesus was who he said he was, we are in big trouble. When
God tore the veil he left the temple. I think we have only
one hope. That is to take out Josiah. We have to try and
kill this movement, and right now he is a key player. If we
can't then we know it's of God. If we can we maintain our

control. It's a huge risk, but it's one we have to take." He turned to his guard and told him to set up an audience with Pilate.

The next morning Pilate was having breakfast with his wife. His centurion walked in. He bowed and then spoke. "Sir! The high priest would like an audience with you." He stood tall at attention and stepped back.

"What does he want?" was the answer that Pilot gave.

"Something about taking out another rabble rouser," the centurion responded.

"I am not in a hurry to put to death another Jew. When I had Jesus of Nazareth put to death it caused huge problems with my wife, her nightmare that night before the judgment had her screaming. My troops are still shaken up by that crucifixion. They are still having terrible dreams about what they have done. The only one not having problems is Patrous. He claims to have been at the tomb when Jesus walked out of it. He told the rest of the guards that Jesus said three words to him. 'You are forgiven.' I really don't know what to make of this. Send him in."

The high priest with his flowing robes with glittering precious stones walked in. He stood before Pilate and asked him to do one thing. "We want that rabble rouser Josiah nailed to a cross. He is getting the people all worked up over this so-called Christ. He is lying to the people about seeing Jesus walk out of the grave. Have you ever heard such a scathing lie in your life? When has anyone ever walked out of a grave?"

Pilate only smiled. "I have a centurion who claims you tried to bribe him to keep quiet. Why should I believe you? My troops know to lie to Rome means death. We know that no one really wants to die."

The high priest's face turned red with anger as he turned and stormed out of Pilate's quarters. He turned back to Pilate. "What will it take for you to nail him to a cross as well?" he asked, then a thought went through his mind. *There is no way I will let that gentile scum keep me from putting an end to that fly named Josiah. He will die. Anyone who tries to make a claim that Jesus was and is God has to go. Our power depends on the people believing that we are the spokesmen for God Almighty. When they try to come against us to stop us we must meet them with total force. The* people *must stay under our control.*

The next morning the sleeping priest rolled over and looked at his sleeping wife beside him. She rolled over looked into his eyes and asked one simple question. "What if this Jesus you killed was who he said he was? What if what this Josiah said is true? What if he and Patrous the Roman centurion were really at the tomb and saw Jesus walk out of the tomb. What if the preaching of Peter and Paul and the other disciples is true? Ask yourself this. Why did the veil closing off the Holy of Holies tear in two the second of Jesus death? If it is because Jesus is who he says he is, then you are fighting against God himself."

As he lay there listening to his wife, the priest's anger grew instantly. "Jesus was not the Messiah. He was a charlatan!" he screamed. "If all the people follow Jesus then we are done as a priesthood!"

"So that's it. You are not interested if Jesus was God incarnate or not. You are interested in protecting your precious priesthood," his wife countered.

The anger the priest was feeling was growing even more intense. "Are you bewitched as well? How can you say such a thing?"

His wife looked at him and said, "I was just repeating what you said. You better be praying a lot. If you are wrong God Almighty will not only take you down, what Jesus said about the temple being torn down, not one stone left upon another will happen. If that happens we are all dead. Remember this, my husband. If you're wrong, you are sowing lies. God is not mocked. God's people's lives and their eternities are at stake. Do you really want to be responsible for God's people not being saved?"

The anger within the Priest exploded. "Even my own wife is deluded by this dead huckster. I will not have you in my presence anymore. Be gone when I get back!" With that pronouncement he left.

She looked around the room and saw her six beautiful children. She looked to heaven and prayed. "Father, in Jesus name I come to you. I really need your help. How am I supposed to take care of these children?"

The priest was walking down the dirt street just outside the temple. He was looking down so not to trip over his own robe. Suddenly he ran into something very hard and big. At first he had thought he had run into a tree, then he looked up. He could hardly see the head of the angel that was right in front of him. "Who, who are you?" he stuttered.

The golden angel looked down on him, smiled broadly, and said, "Gabriel."

The priest turned ghost white. "Am I going to die, am I going to heaven?" he asked with a voice that was totally terrorized.

Gabriel with a little chuckle put it to him straight. "First, with what you have been doing to God's people I am afraid the place you would find yourself is quite warm. Before God drops you into the pits of hell, he will watch the flames lick at the bottom of your feet for what you have done. The Jewish people, because of where you are leading them, are going to be in exile for two thousand years. Israel will once again be a powerful nation. But you will never live to see it. And when the end comes you will be in hell."

The priest dropped to his knees in tears. "What must I do to be saved?"

Gabriel only had to say one thing. "Believe on the Lord Jesus Christ and be baptized in the Name of the Father and of the Son and of the Holy Spirit and you will be saved."

With that the priest dropped to his knees and prayed and received Jesus Christ as his Savior and Lord. When he walked back into his home and his wife shuddered in fear. I had a meeting today. The angel Gabriel and I had a meeting. He convinced me that believing in Christ was a wise thing to do. I am now a believer in the Christ of God. I don't know what the reaction of my fellow priests, but I know it won't be pretty.

21
......

The Final Cross

The next day he walked into the temple. He saw several of his colleagues storming around the chambers.
The chief priest, angry once again, could not stop screaming. "Those crosses, I keep seeing those crosses all over the
city. We have to put an end to Josiah. He must be nailed
to a cross as well."

The priest looked at the high priest. "I think you are
making a huge mistake. I ran into Gabriel today.
That angel must have been ten feet tall. I accepted Christ
myself. I am afraid you are wrong. Jesus died and walked
out of the grave; that I am convinced of."

The high priest became even angrier. "I will not give
up control over the people. I want to enjoy the office God
put me into. I can't do that with another rabble rouser." He
then turned to one of his guards, handed him one hundred
pieces of silver, and told him to go bribe Pilate.

The guard walked into Pilate's palace. He walked up
tohim and simply said, "The high priest wants Josiah out

of here." He handed him the one hundred pieces of silver and left. . . . . . .

xxxxx

Josiah left his quarters and walked outside. The air was fresh, yet something did not see just right. It was as though his world was about to crash around him, he did not quite understand it, yet he did. He had been making many enemies among the priesthood for the last few years. His cross necklaces had been making their way around believer's necks. People had been accepting The Christ and his salvation. The more people received God's salvation, the madder the
priesthood became as they saw their power over the people becoming less and less. They knew Paul was preaching the priesthood of the believers even from prison, making the priest even more angry because they could not silence him. Then one morning it happened just as it had the morning they broke into Josiah's house demanding the cross for the Christ. But this day would be one in which Josiah would spend it with his friends. It would be a day of fulfillment and enjoyment. They would sit and listen to John's teachings on love and compassion of Christ and how important it was to have that love in their lives so they could share it with others.

Josiah, as he sat and listened to John, noticed Anna across the way. He started to get up to walk over to her. She saw him, shook her head, and turned away. Josiah shook his head and stopped cold in his tracks. At the end of the study he did not want to leave. It was as though this would be his last study. This would be the last time he would ever see his brothers and sisters in Christ.

He did not understand it at that time, but knew somehow he would soon. Finally, very late that night he left and went back to his home.

That night Josiah dreamt of Anna. He could see her walking through a field of clover. He could see her big brown eyes, and her smile glisten in the sunlight. She held out her hand to her just as his door crashed open. The temple guard attacked and started striking him.

First in the head, and then in the ribs. He was spitting up blood. The pain was intense as he forced himself to stand. He no sooner got to his feet than he was hit in the back of his head by a huge piece of dogwood. He went back down to his knees.

A Roman soldier grabbed him, stood him up, and said. "C'mon, cross boy. You built lots of these for us to kill your people with, you have got to have one more of those death trees in your barn for us to nail you to."

Josiah, still spitting blood, shook his head trying to get it clear. He knew he had one more in the stable. He just did not want to get nailed to it. The Romans forced him to walk out to the barn. He opened the door slowly. They saw the last cross. It was straight and strong. And they knew they were going to nail him to it.

They then tied it to his back and forced him to climb Golgotha to the same place the Christ was nailed to a tree.

Josiah looked up to the heavens. Raised one finger to point to the Lord on his throne, he said only one thing. "Here I come, Jesus. Please use the crosses I have out there to be touching your people. And please get a message to Anna that I still need to be forgiven."

* * *

Anna was just starting to walk out of father's house. Patrous ran up to her. "Anna, they have taken Josiah and are about to nail him to a cross."

Anna froze in her tracks. The Holy Spirit brought it to her mind the one thing she had to do. She had not forgiven Josiah for killing her brother. She realized that her time was short and headed for the hill. She had to be there and see Josiah hang on a cross and die. She had to let him know before he died that yes she does forgive him for killing her brother. She knew she had to forgive him for what he had done. She knew that because of what Christ did on the Cross she had been forgiven. She could do no less for Josiah.

* * *

They tied Josiah's wrist to the tree, and then as they drove the first nail into the palm of his hand, his scream could be heard for miles. He had never felt such intense pain in his life. They then pulled his other hand to the left side of the cross. They tied it securely and then drove the nail. They then raised the cross and dropped it into the hole to hold it. The cross was secured and Josiah was left to hang on the cross until he died on that tree that he had built.

The sun was hot and dehydration set in quickly. They did not want him to die too quick so water was given to him on a sponge. He took it and shook his head. The first hour went by, then the second, then the third.

Each hour seemed like an eternity. He would try to raise himself up to breath, the pain would become more intense, he would lower himself down and then could not breathe. He looked out and shook his head. Was he dreaming? Was it real. Was that Anna? It was. Was she coming to gloat because he was getting the same kind of death that her brother received from another cross that he had built? All he knew was that she was the most beautiful thing that had ever come into his life. And he blew it because of his love of money more than loyalty to his people.

Anna, in tears, walked to the base of Josiah's cross. With tears in her eyes, she looked up at Josiah. She wanted to take him down from the cross. She put her hand on the cross around her neck that he had made. With a week smile she looked at Josiah on the Cross. She found herself saying, "Josiah, I was wrong. I should have forgiven you long ago. Can you find it in your heart to forgive me? I do forgive you, Josiah. I love you."

The only strength that Josiah could find was enough just to nod his head and break a weak smile. He had heard the words he had longed to hear forever. He knew his time was very short. He looked off into the distance. He could hardly believe his eyes. Jesus the Christ was walking toward him. Jesus held his hand out as Josiah was released from the cross to walk with Christ forever.

* * *

The next day Anna sat in her room crying profusely. She had seen the man that she could have loved die because of the crosses that he had made for years after the death and resurrection of Christ to show believers and nonbelievers as well their commitment to Christ. There was a knock at the door. Her Father answered and called her. She walks to the door and sees Patrous. "Anna, I think it is imperative that we continue on with what Josiah started. He has the shop set up for making those small crosses for people to identify other believers. Would you be willing to help me with that endeavor?"

Her answer was quick. "Absolutely. But first give me a day to really get my head where it needs to be."

Patrous smiled and walked away to return the next day.

* * *

She left her room and went for a long walk and prayed. As she prayed, she came to realize a truth. All people had sinned. She then realized a truth that once again drove her to her knees to ask for forgiveness. That truth was simple.

Patrous and Anna would work together for the rest of their lives working on crosses. Their son Josiah would become an evangelist who would draw thousands of people to the Christ.

Remember this. We have all built the cross!

Made in the USA
Monee, IL
04 September 2022